T0156650

NIGHT SHIFTERS III

The Great War

Cheryl Lee

Order this book online at www.trafford.com
or email orders@trafford.com

Most Trafford titles are also available at major online book retailers.

© Copyright 2018 Cheryl Lee.
All rights reserved. No part of this publication may be reproduced, stored in a retrieval system, or transmitted, in any form or by any means, electronic, mechanical, photocopying, recording, or otherwise, without the written prior permission of the author.

Print information available on the last page.

ISBN: 978-1-4907-9204-0 (sc)
ISBN: 978-1-4907-9205-7 (hc)
ISBN: 978-1-4907-9211-8 (e)

Library of Congress Control Number: 2018963967

Because of the dynamic nature of the Internet, any web addresses or links contained in this book may have changed since publication and may no longer be valid. The views expressed in this work are solely those of the author and do not necessarily reflect the views of the publisher, and the publisher hereby disclaims any responsibility for them.

Any people depicted in stock imagery provided by Getty Images are models, and such images are being used for illustrative purposes only.
Certain stock imagery © Getty Images.

Trafford rev. 11/17/2018

www.trafford.com

North America & international
toll-free: 1 888 232 4444 (USA & Canada)
fax: 812 355 4082

Contents

Chapter One

Daring Rescue

Running as fast as we could, I could see a line forming up a head. Eyes peeking through the night I knew we were headed right into danger. Then with in an instant our bodies shifted becoming one with then night. Eric transformed into some kind of night warrior. Not only was he transforming, I transformed as well.

Strong power surges ran through my body, me feet were not even touching the ground. I don't know how we plowed through the shifters, but we did, others joined in with us.

A fast-moving white mist guided us deeper into the woods where we could hear loud screaming. Sounds of wolves growling and howling, was all around us. We came to a part of the woods near a huge rock near tall shrubs and hid behind them.

We watched as people were dancing around a fire, singing out to a warrior of the night.

Nai'okah was lying on a flat slab of rock that appeared to be a sacrificial table. Her arms were bleeding and her blood dripped into bowls beneath her. Just as I saw in my vision two white eyes emerged from the darkness only they were painted on a man's chest. He wore huge bear skin and the head was like a mask covering his face.

"Who is this mysterious man?"

I asked myself.

Then it hit me.

"Jeremy Hawk!"

My blood boiled and burned deep within me as I watched this ritual. Jeremy walks up to up to Nai'okah staring down at her. She was terrified, both Eric and I were ready to make our move when a huge white wolf came and stood between us. It was the biggest wolf I had ever seen. But there was something about this wolf that seemed quite different.

Looking deep into my eyes it spoke to me, telling me to wait. I looked over at Eric; his hand gripped a huge knife on his side. I cautioned him to wait. We watched in horror as this man stood over her picking up one of the bowls. Holding it up into the air he called upon a spirit but not just any spirit a very evil one.

"Great spirit of the night, I call upon you to accept my sacrifice, Oh dark and powerful one I offer up her blood and her soul to you."

The white wolf next me growled deeply, I watched as it clutched the earth with its huge paws. Never taking its eyes off Jeremy we watched a mist of darkness circled above Jeremy's head. He invited the evil spirit to rest in his body as he prepared to drink Nai'okah's blood.

By this time more wolves joined us and were ready for battle. Sounds of growls, and cracking sounds like bones breaking was all around us. Once Jeremy swallowed her blood the dark mist consumed his body.

He screamed as if he was in pain, but then Jeremy was no longer Jeremy he was someone else or perhaps I should say something.

The people around him fell to the ground worshipping the night shifter, I had a gut feeling I knew what the wolves were waiting for. As soon as the creature takes human form they will strike. I could see the silhouette of a man's body inside the dark mist. Once the creature was fully formed using Jeremy's body the sound of growling increased around me.

Picking up the bowl of blood the night shifter proceeded to drink Nai'okah's blood. Looking down at her it spoke.

"Your blood line is very strong, rich and full of power, you will do well."

Picking up a huge knife, he raised it above his head, spoke in a native language and before he could carry out his attack on her life. The wolves sprang into action. One by one they attacked. Pouncing on the shifter like a ton of bricks. The dark mist quickly exited the Jeremy's body. The wolves ripped him into pieces, I dared not to look.

Eric and I rushed over to Nai'okah's side; she was unconscious and still bleeding. We had to act fast; there was no way I could shift with her like this. We carried her as we ran as fast as we could through the woods, the smell of her blood was attracting more than just shifters, but something else.

There was no time to look back, only forward. A pack of wolves acted as our escorts but something hovered over us.

Then one by one the wolves disappeared, swallowed by the night the battle raged on. I remembered in my vision how I pulled something out of my pouch. Looking around I could see wolves half revealed, fighting the darkness.

Eric and I kept running but I had to do something. We had to act in seconds in order to create a barrier between us and the shifter. However, carrying Nai'okah made it very difficult.

The wolves were fighting as hard as they could, when more joined in the fight, we used it to our advantage. With only seconds to spare, I told Eric to create a barrier, just as I saw in my vision, he quickly drew a circle around us and then dropped sacred stones on the ground. I held Nai'okah in my arms until he was finished.

Then we switched off and I took powder from my pouch tossing it into the air. It sizzled, and then the smell of burnt flesh hit my nose. Although the wolves fought hard, some of them never returned from the darkness. The night seemed to bleed and spill on the ground.

Once we were covered, it was time get moving again, I held Nai'okah while Eric dropped stones on the ground. We were covered by an invisible barrier that protected us. Covered in Nai'okah's blood, it was hard to keep away any hungry beast. She started to moan a little, which was a good sign; uttering only a few words I could feel her will to live.

We were only moments away from the clearing when we saw a pack of wolves up ahead. One by one they appeared, side by side they stood. Eric and I kept going and did not stop.

It was hard to tell if they were on our side or not, at this point I didn't care. Nai'okah needed medical treatment and fast, so Eric and I pressed on and headed straight for them.

The closer we got to the edge the more the wolves moved in, my heart fluttered and the smell of burnt flesh was very strong in the air. We pushed our bodies as far as they could go. Keeping our stride together, Eric and I held on to Nai'okah with all our might.

Then out of know where something pushed us, and down we went. Nai'okah's body hit the ground hard.

A strong force moved in between us forcing us to drop her, as we looked up dark ripples in the night hovered above us. Just as it got closer the wolves moved in, I thought for sure this was going to be the end of us. Surely these massive beasts were going to have their way with us.

Then the appearance huge claw like hands came out from beyond the darkness to pick up Nai'okah. And just as it did, the wolves attacked. Tearing off a limb of the beast.

Although we were surrounded; we hurried to get to Nai'okah out, the wolves fought to keep the evil away from us.

Trying to get to our pouches as we ran, I yelled out to Eric.

"We must get to the clearing and fast."

Eric agreed. Just when he reached for his pouch, something grabbed his legs from behind. He screamed out for help, I tried to get to him before the darkness could swallow him up. I leaped as far as I could and grabbed hold of his hands.

"Brother, don't let me go!"

Eric screamed.

"Hold on tight and don't let go!"

I pulled and pulled until we were holding on to each other's shoulders, Eric kept screaming, as the dark entity pulled him deeper, there was no time I had to do something to save my brother.

I quickly reached into his pouch pulled out the sacred stones and tossed them into the darkness. Bright lights shot out like firecrackers, the shifter began to go from a dark mist, to a hideous looking wolf, and its body sizzled loud as it was burning. The sound it made pierced my ears.

Once it let go of Eric, I could see inside of it somehow, I could not take my eyes off of it. Eric pulled on my arm telling me to go.

Looking into the eyes of the beast it was paralyzing. Even though I saw deep within its soul, I also saw what used to be a man. A man whose life was overtaken by a dark entity, consumed then transformed.

The more I stared, Eric pulled on me, then I felt massive arms yanked me away from what I was deeply caught up into. Shaking my head, trying to snap out of it, Big John spoke to me.

"Come on son we must leave now!"

Once we reached the edge of the woods, others greeted us. They quickly took Nai'okah away, while we were taken to the council of the Elders. I thanked Big John for saving me, and then Eric thanked me for saving his life. Big John told us to thank him later; there was no time to talk.

Chief Spearhorn was waiting for us, he told me that my friends were safe, and were taken home. I looked around for my uncle Benjamin but could not see him, Chief Spearhorn stated that my uncle was safe, and he had asked him to take care of Tony and Elsha. Chief Spearhorn was full of gratitude, but I was full of questions.

"What am I?"

I did not want to waste any more time with riddles, parables or puzzles. And to my surprise Chief Spearhorn said neither did he.

Once we were inside the council building, two men were posted outside of the door. Chief Spearhorn began to talk about the horrific event that took place. First the Chief looked at me and then Eric, examining us with his eyes. Then he sat down and a told us that we are favored among the spirit guides.

I felt my blood began to boil again so I questioned him once more.

"What the hell am I!"

Chief Spearhorn quickly responded.

"Centuries ago there were many like you, when I was a young boy my father told me of a story about a very powerful being sent by the spirit guides to protect our people. Some called them night angel, because he had the ability to transform himself and blend with the night."

I wondered how he became to be that way, but Chief Spearhorn went on explaining.

"My ancestors called him night angel, one who walks with the night. Although no one knows how he came to be but my father described him as tall, broad shoulder, hair black very silky. His features are brown skinned, dark brown eyes. Legend says he blends with the elements of earth, a gift from the spirit guides."

Chapter Two

DESCENDANTS

Chief Spearhorn went on telling us how some believed this night angel was good and others thought of him as evil. There had been talks that he could be a skin walker. No one really knew, then Eric stepped forward scolding the Elders.

"Was this another one of your tests, to prove that we are brave enough for you? Why give us these pouches and tell us to use them when we felt the urge to!"

Chief Spearhorn quickly responded in a very stern voice.

"You are who you are; there are things I don't need to tell you because you already know. Both of you possess powers that are beyond this world, none that no one has ever seen. You would have not believed me if I would have told you."

"The only way was for both of you to join and let destiny take its course. I had faith in both of you that one day you would figure it out. I didn't want it to be face to face with danger."

Then Chief Spearhorn requested that Eric and I be taken to his cabin, I was so tired of all of the games, and the waiting was killing me. Eric was very upset; I think he was just as tired as I was.

Sitting in Chief Spearhorn's cabin was not the place I wanted to be. Eric stared out of the window motionless as I paced the floor. I wanted to see my friends but not before I got some answers.

My mind was filled with such confusion, I could hardly think straight. As we waited for the Chief, I tried to grab hold of who I was, but the real question is what and not who. I thought about Nai'okah and wondered how she was doing.

Her life will never be the same again; come to think of it all of us are different now. Eric stayed close to the window, I got a little curious

As I walked toward him, I wanted to see why he was staring out of the window.

He spoke softly spoke.

"Someone is coming, I can't tell who it is, but I know she's female."

I wondered how he knew, because it was so dark outside. But my instincts told me as well. There came a knock at the door.

We both looked at each other, walking toward the door. Ms. Creed entered. She had a look of relief on face.

"Boys I'm glad to see both of you are safe."

She hugged us both, as she shook nervously. I gave her some assurance.

"We are good, how are you?"

She took off her coat, and said she was a total wreck. Eric asked if she heard anything, she said only that Chief Spearhorn asked her to wait here with us.

Eric and I couldn't wait for the Chief, so we started asking Ms. Creed questions about what she heard or saw. She seemed quite disturbed, but as strong as she was, she kept her composure.

Ms. Creed said there had been some strange sightings around the reservation tonight, she was kept in one of the buildings with Elsha and Tony which she told me they were safe and how they left hours ago. She continued telling us that we must remain on the reservation until further notice. I didn't like it.

"So, what are we prisoners now? What about my family?"

Ms. Creed assured me that they were fine, but for me not to worry. Ms. Creed continued to explain to us how strange sounds came from the woods began to frighten those around her. Not knowing what was going on men stood on guard at the door. The wind picked up strong as if a storm was brewing. Ms. Creed stated she heard a commotion and went to ask but of course Elsha was right by her side.

Ms. Creed told her story.

"As I sat with the children, Elsha was doing a good job by telling them stories, and Tony was very entertaining as well being silly with them. I wanted to know what was happening outside, so I stepped out into the hall. One of the men named Donavon told me I would be safer if I remained inside. When I asked him what he meant by safe he said they found the missing girl, but her capturer was still on the loose."

Eric and I looked at each other we knew that couldn't be true because we saw him die. Ms. Creed continued……

"Just as Donavon was talking, I stared over his shoulder to see a young woman carried on a stretcher, her blood-soaked clothes startled me. Donavon told me to stay inside and not to come out. As I waited until he was gone, I did some investigating on my own. I wanted to know where they took her, so I followed the trail of blood."

Eric and I both wanted to know her status. Ms. Creed said she was alive but unconscious. The tribal doctors and nurses were working on her when something weird happened. Eric shifted in his seat.

"What do you mean by weird?"

Ms. Creed paused for a moment, the she continued…

"Keeping my distance, I stepped into an adjourning room where I could see her, then she started choking, I saw her body shake, as the nurses tried cleaning her wounds. Nai'okah screamed. He father was talking to her encouraging her to hold on. He was later escorted out, to a nearby waiting room. She was given a shot to relax her. Once she calmed, everyone left, and I went in. She appeared to be sleeping so when I got closer to her, she opened her eyes"

At this point she couldn't continue the look in her face was very grim. While in his chair, Eric leaned forward asking her.

"What did you see?"

Ms. Creed took a deep breath and replied.

"Death, she had death in her eyes."

A cold chill came over me; I looked at Ms. Creed to inquire more.

"What was the color of her eyes?"

Ms. Creed gasped for air, and then she softly responded.

"Black, they were black."

Clutching her silver stone, she leaned back, and sighed. Then she looked at me asking me a question that brought back horrifying memories.

"What was it like? Do you remember anything after your rescue?"

I hesitated to answer her, but I did anyway.

"You lay in the balance between heaven and earth, the spirit guides are with you, but evil is there also, Nai'okah said she felt she was being followed and she wanted me to help her. I will never get over the fear she had in her eyes."

Eric was tired of waiting for the Chief to arrive, I asked Ms. Creed if she had any updates on Nai'okah and she hesitated to speak again. By this time Eric asked if there was anything else that happened in the room Ms. Creed looked at me with tears almost streaming down her face.

"Will she survive it, whatever has her I fear she gone past this world. She's still alive last I heard but her eyes were like a dark hole, I struggled to tear myself away from looking at her. I couldn't stop staring at her; the only thing that broke my trance was a noise on the other side of the door. She just laid there still so I ran out through another door."

I think it is time we all came pretty clear with each other, as Ms. Creed spoke, I thought about the darkness when Eric was pulled half way into it. I saw deep inside the shifter, then I saw him as a man. Within seconds I saw his life and his death. He was once a warrior that defied Liwanu, because of that he was killed, his soul devoured, and he was transformed into a hideous beast. His soul bound to evil for all eternity. As for Ms. Creed's question Eric gave her the answer.

"She will survive if she is one of the chosen, unfortunately he has tasted her blood, and she will have to endure total darkness. If she survives her blood will return natural, but if it doesn't, she will now be an enemy."

Ms. Creed seemed puzzled by this so turned to me. The urgency in her voice had also puzzled me.

"When you survived your attack, what happened to you? I mean really what did you experience?"

I just looked at her and told her she didn't want to know; besides I don't even know if I could. Ms. Creed insisted that I tell her. She had such a frightful look in her eyes.

Eric approaches her.

"What is really going on with you? Why this sudden urgency to know what happens after an attack?

Nai "okah was not attacked by an animal, well technically she was but she was cut by a knife and she lost a lot of blood."

She quickly responds.

"No something else happened to her, she was examined from head to toe, when I looked into her eyes, they were black as night. She told me….."

She stopped in midsentence clutching her stone necklace. Eric questioned her again.

"When we rescued her, she was bleeding very badly, Kyle and I saw her being cut, so what are you talking about, where is she can you take us to her?"

Chapter Three

DARKER SECRETS

I had to agree with him, if there is more going on with Nai'okah we needed to know, we did our best to protect her. The only way she could be turned is if she was injured or perhaps…my mind went back to the life of the warrior I saw.

As a human he defied Liwanu he was forced to drink the blood of his own people then he stared into the eyes of the fierce one while thick black mist surrounded him. I can recall having the same experience.

Eric was right we needed to get to her. Which also questioned why would chief want us to wait here? Why send Ms. Creed? Both of us just had to know.

"Why are you so worried what happened in that room?"

Ms. Creed nearly choked then she said that she could no longer keep her secret. Looking at me then at Eric made us swear we would help her once she revealed her secret. She was not joking she nearly shouted at us.

"When I was in the room with Nai'okah, before she opened her eyes, she knew I was there, only it wasn't her but something else that knew me. Whatever it is, it does not want me it said it wanted Nai'Jae. And that he was waiting for her."

Eric and I looked at each other and asked.

"Who is Nai'Jae?"

Struggling to talk Ms. Creed shocked us both.

She's.....she's my daughter.

She buried her face in her hands and explained how she has been hiding her daughter. She dreaded this day would ever come. She keeps her away because she is afraid something will happen to her. I couldn't give her an answer but all I could tell her was that she needed to be strong.

"When the beast drinks your blood, it gives him more power, when he takes your life, he devours your soul. What else are you not telling us?"

Eric intervened.

"Yes Ms. Creed we have to know, perhaps we can help."

The nightmares have started, my mother says she been screaming out in the middle of the night. My parents say she is sometimes locked in, she can't wake up and when she does, terror is in her eyes. I have requested my parents take her far away and keep her away until I can figure something out. So Elsha was right she is a woman with a secret.

Ms. Creed sat and told us about her daughter, she had very good reason to protect her. I asked her why the fascination with genealogy.

"My fascination with genealogy is because I love to do it and find the connection to the blood lines. My lineage runs very deep; I stay close to the Spearhorns for many reasons.

First of all, we are related in some ways and second, I stayed close because I feel protected. Many of us have dark secrets some even darker. But these are the darker secrets of my life protecting my daughter all of these years."

Now we understood how she felt. We thought perhaps we should tell her the truth about what happened in the woods. And about the strange thing that happened to us, but before we could Chief Spearhorn, Benjamin, and Big John entered the room.

Chief Spearhorn addressed us.

"I apologize for having you wait for so long, you have had an eventful night, so the time has come for more truths."

He ushered us to sit down and then he began to tell us about the evil that has plagued our land claimed the life of ten men tonight. Before we could ask about Nai'okah, he said she was in a coma, and is under twenty-four-hour care. With his cane he held it upward and spoke in his native language.

"It is time for you both to know, the power of the eagle. Its eyes can see far beyond any mans eye; its wing can stretch far beyond any mans arms. Centuries ago my forefathers talked of visions of seeing an ancient one high in the mountains. They heard many stories about a journey where men dreaded to go. One day my forefathers made a decree those children born in their time would have sacred prayers spoken over them for protection. Once they become of age they are taken to sacred grounds known as the Canyon of Souls. It is a place where the winds blow strong. Some say when the ancient eagle flaps its wings the winds blow fierce, you can hear the cries of the people. Legend says it is the home of an ancient bird who keeps watch over the land.

My great grandfather was among them. It is said the eagle's eyes glowed like diamonds. Some thought it was the spirit guides inhabiting the bird to communicate with the living. Many tried to go there to seek wisdom but never returned. It lived high up in the cliffs and it was about a three-day journey to get to.

Only the young warriors were to go alone, they could take nothing with them, but they had to climb the mountain with only the support of each other. When they reached the cliff, they were met by a guardian and could only enter one at a time.

Screeching sounds came from within the cave, the others seemed frightened. When it was time for my great grandfather, he met the eagle face to face, it was not an eagle but a man, dressed as an eagle but eyes of crystal blue.

Only the chosen one could see the true form of the ancient one. His skin was dark toned, and he bore the symbols of our ancient language.

I interrupted him for a moment.

"I too have seen this man in my dreams, each time he saved my life. Chief why do you keep telling us these stories when so many around us are dying? No disrespect but I am beyond tired at this point we should be coming up with a solution instead of ghost stories."

Eric also stated he also saw the same man in his dreams. And he was ready to get more answers, we turned to Ms. Creed and she couldn't recall, although she too had heard of this man. I could tell by the way he gripped the head of his cane our actions were upsetting him.

"I know this is a difficult time for all of us, what took place today was something most unbelievable. Surely you are the chosen ones guided by the great spirits to help defeat the enemy.

Calm your storms there is great work ahead. You are not like the other but different you have the power within you to combine with the elements. I'm sorry I could not tell you this before I had to wait for the right time."

He step forward placing his hands on our chests.

"Follow your instincts, let them guide you."

The urgency in his voice was very serious, but it still didn't give me what I wanted. If this is the man that we have been seeing is real, I'm glad he is on our side. But it still doesn't explain what I am.

My brother and I can do the unthinkable then together we can put an end to this madness. I grabbed my coat and headed towards the door. Chief Spearhorn didn't want me to leave, Eric followed as well as Ms. Creed.

"Please stay, don't go yet there is much more I have to say. Besides it's not safe out there."

Not wanting to be disrespectful I had to leave, but it was a chance I was willing to take. I wanted to know about Nai'okah, so I told him that I must leave to clear my head.

But what I really wanted is to find Nai'okah and talk to her somehow. And besides I needed to call my parents and check on Becca. Chief Spearhorn encouraged us to come back however he understood our decision to leave.

Eric asked Ms. Creed to show us where she last saw Nai'okah, we told Chief Spearhorn that we would return. The three of us headed out towards the medical clinic. No one spoke; Eric kept his eye on the woods.

Owls hooting off in the night echoed through the trees. Ms. Creed was walking in between us, I could sense her emotions. She was scared but more so for her daughter, I gave a smile and told her not to worry.

We arrive at the medical center which was still heavily guarded, thinking that we were not going to get in. A few guards approached us asking the nature of our business. We told them we needed to see a sick friend.

Ms. Creed kindly asked him to let up pass, he didn't budge and neither did we. I could feel agitation coming from Eric, the sounds of knuckles cracking somewhat startled the man.

Eric gave him a creepy stare; something in my brother's eyes moved the man without question. He moved aside to let us pass. As soon as we entered the building, I could feel her, I don't know how but I sensed Eric caught it as well. Headed in the direction where we sensed Nai'okah.

Ms. Creed was puzzled.

"Why are we going this way? Her room is on the other side."

Eric replied.

"They have moved her she's not there anymore."

We walked down a long corridor toward the back and entered a room marked private. She was alone and unconscious still. Ms. Creed walked toward her softly calling out to her.

"Nai'okah, Nai'okah."

We stepped forward and, looking at her I knew what to do. I asked Ms. Creed to give me her necklace and before she could raise an eyebrow, I asked her to trust me.

I took the necklace and before I could place it on her forehead Chief Spearhorn entered the room while his guard kept watch at the door.

"I knew I would find you here; don't be alarmed, I know what you are attempting to do. The four corners prayer works with four people. Let's begin."

Chief Spearhorn took his place on the left side of the bed representing the east. I stood at her right side representing the west, Eric at her feet representing the south and Ms. Creed stood at the top of her bed representing the north. Placing the silver stone on her forehead, the stone turned black then back to silver. We were all shocked Ms. Creed inquired.

"Why is it doing that?

Chief Spearhorn quickly responded.

"She is in between worlds; her life is the balance now."

Just as he kept talking the stone turned black again Eric was getting impatient, but Chief Spearhorn told all of us to keep calm and focus. He said this is going to take us coming together to go into the darkness to retrieve her. He said we must keep our minds clear, looking at Ms. Creed he stated.

"Be strong, keep your head clear, and keep the stone on her forehead it will help to lead her back."

She nervously nodded, and Ms. Creed kept her focus. Looking at Eric and then at me he told us not to let our ears deceive us. There is an unbalance in the atmosphere, so we must all be strong.

"We will enter into a realm filled with darkness, hear what she hears, and see what sees. Fear is not an option so cleanse your thoughts now."

I knew what he meant; I had been there before it is not a fun place. I too recited the sacred prayer; Ms. Creed trembled as she held stone over Nai'okah's head. While Chief Spearhorn held his cane over her body, the crystal eyes of the eagle glowed brightly.

Speaking in native language he said a prayer, and then he laid the cane across her body. The room grew cold as dark shadows circled us. Chief Spearhorn called her name softly telling her to focus on his voice.

We each laid hands on her as a point of contact we let our bodies transcend us into another place beyond our world. The smell of burnt flesh was in the air, more voices joined in as we journeyed to find her.

There was total darkness, eerie sounds circled us we could not see each other. Screams pierced through dark there was no sign of light anywhere. Remembering what Chief Spearhorn said I kept reciting the prayer in my head.

But I kept hearing a voice of someone crying.

It was the voice of a small child crying out for help in the darkness.

"Help me, mommy please help me! Grandma, Grandpa, where are you? The dark man is coming; he's coming to get me! Please Great Spirits don't let me die!"

The screams were so loud; I had no choice but to turn my attention towards them. My gut told me to keep searching. As if I were pulled into another world through the one I just entered.

I followed the sounds until I heard the screams again. Moving closer I could see an image of a small child, she was wondering through the dark screaming and she was scared. Flashes of white light flashed in and out of the dark like lightening.

Somehow this felt different I'm not in the same place as they were; I was in someone else's nightmare but whose nightmare I wondered.

When I found him, I told him not to be afraid he kept calling for his mother. He circled as if he didn't see me. All I could do was to watch in horror as an even darker figure appeared.

He was tall broad, arms long and massive. I watched a long slimy tongue came out of its mouth moving up and down the boy's arm.

Its wolf like appearance was hideous for the child to look upon. He screamed again with tears running down his face.

Taking another look at the child I realized the child was me. I was helpless and powerless. This must have been a suppressed memory of my youth. This was just a distraction of my childhood fears; I was not going to let this stop my mission. Just as a child that is helpless and defenseless, I had to press pass this.

I should have listened to Chief Spearhorn and heeded to his advice. He said to stay focused that I would hear and see what Nai'okah would see and hear.

I turned my energy toward the dark and focused as hard as I could, the lights kept flashing in threes, but each time they flashed I was able to see the little boy more clearly.

A beast lay over him tasting his skin. Extending its long teeth, it set out to kill the child. Within seconds I was upon this beast, wresting with it, every strike I made was like bolts of lightning tearing its flesh. The beast let out a loud cry, and charge at me again, striking my arm leaving claw marks. Then with one final blow, the beast was no more.

The little boy lay sweating, in his sleep, her heart beating fast, whispering to him I calmed his young spirit.

"There now, you are safe he won't bother you anymore. Rest well."

This is what I needed to free the inner child and release the nightmare. Now I knew how to free Nai'okah.

Searching through the darkness, I heard moaning, I followed the sound until I reached her.

Then I saw her, bound by terror, feared by her nightmares. A sleek silhouette of a dark entity hovered over smothering her. I had to act fast but before I sensed my brother and Chief Spearhorn.

Dust crystals immediately covered the dark entity as if someone had thrown them. I knew my brother was there.

"Go brother quickly!"

I quickly moved to get Nai'okah before the dark entity could return again.

As I approached her, I whispered I was real and was there to get her out. I encourage her that I was real and was there to get her out.

Following the streaks of light, I screamed at her to wake up, I picked her up and carried her toward the light. While screaming at her to wake up, I was pulled from behind, the lights were dimming but I had to press on.

She was not going to be stuck in darkness; I fought through until I reached a lighted door and threw Nai'okah in. I immediately followed, hearing the voice of another child that was all too familiar.

I turned before the door close to see a young girl reaching for me.

Awakened by my brother standing over me I was back in Nai'okah's room.

"Welcome back brother, I thought I was going to have to go in and rescue you.

I asked about Nai'okah but Eric said he would explain later.

Kyle said he would explain later, but then she walked in.

This was not over someone else is in there and she needs my help. Eric wondered who it could be, he asked me if I knew who it was, I hesitated.

Then I said.

"Nai'jae."

Chapter Four

Locked In

Chief Spearhorn asked if I was sure it was Nai'jae.

I replied.

"Yes, I remember seeing her in a photo at Ms. Creed's house. I'm afraid she has been targeted and her nightmares will now become a reality."

Chief Spearhorn rubbed his chin and sighed.

"You two prepare to go home, I will inform Ms. Creed, of this. I think it would be best if it comes from me. Eric why don't you travel with your brother, Kyle I hope your parents won't mind. The two of you together are very strong. Don't worry about Nai'okah we will watch over her."

Eric and I planned to leave as Ms Creed entered her eyes full of tears. She told the Chief how she must leave to go to her little girl. She asked me what I saw, and Chief said he would explain. I just couldn't walk away from here knowing what I know. I asked the Chief to allow me to explain it to her my way.

He agreed.

I told Ms. Creed that I entered Nai'jae's nightmare to console her. I explained to her how at first, I didn't know it was her daughter until the darkness cleared. Continuing on I told her how Nai'Jae was asleep and her heart rate lowered.

"I spoke to her in her dream, the beast that came for her I attacked and killed. She was covered in a white mist then disappeared. The chief is right you are going to have to be strong for her, she needs you."

Ms. Creed was shaken but, yet she remained strong. She thought by keeping her daughter away she would be safe. Patagonia was the last place she wanted her daughter to be. She told us that she would leave first thing in the morning.

I called my parents and told them that I was on my way home and asked if it was okay for Eric to come with me for awhile. Dad thought that would be a good idea since he needed some help organizing the garage.

Benjamin phoned and stated he would pick us up in an hour. I also called Elsha and Tony, neither one of them answered. I asked the chief about Nai'okah and what he thinks we should do. He said he will keep a 24-hour watch on her. I also asked if he thinks she will recover.

"That depends on her fight and will to live, I have a strange feeling she is needed more in the Spirit World than down here in the land of the living. Nai'okah is locked in."

Eric quickly replied.

"What do you mean by locked in?"

Chief said he would explain on the way back to his place. While we walked, he told us how he feels that Nai'okah is in a place where she can't return from until the time is right. He mentioned since we are approaching the time of the great gathering of eagles.

He strongly felt she will return when the time calls for it. I had almost forgotten about the gathering. I know it's going to be somewhere in the west but where?

Then it hit me, from one of my visions where the rock meets the sky, I repeated it multiple times in my head.

And then an overwhelming feeling came over me within a flash I saw eagles flying toward the western sky, on their back were angel like beings. They moved toward a huge rock that reached the heavens.

Perched high on the mountain is the dark man with the crystal blue eyes. He's seems to be summoning everyone. That is where we must journey to as well.....Wyoming.

Once we returned to Chiefs cabin, he encouraged us to keep in touch with him. While we waited for Benjamin, I packed my suitcase, all sorts of thoughts ran through my mind about Ms. Creeds daughter. I really hope she remains safe. But in the meantime, Eric and I had to a lot to catch up on. When Benjamin arrived, we headed back home.

Somehow, I felt I would soon return to the reservation. But I also felt a pull in another direction, clutching my chest I sighed.

"Nephew are you alright? Is everything okay?"

I just looked at him and told him I was fine. The events that played in my head caused me to take in a deep breath. I felt more like an anxiety attack.

"I'm okay uncle, just a mild anxiety attack."

He too sighed then he explained how he felt our pain. He advised me to keep my mind clear of thoughts. He also told us not to speak about the events that took place. He said my family has permission to visit the reservation whenever they choose as long as they announce their visit.

We talked more as we headed home. Benjamin told us how he too felt the pull to head west. He said in due time we will meet. The gathering will take place soon and we must be ready.

Eric wondered about it as well.

"What do you suppose will happen there?"

Benjamin just said calmly.

"I don't know, but time will tell. Some of our brothers and sisters have already started their journey. Every year there is a great gathering of eagles. But this year will be different. The moon will be just as big, Earth and sky will come close to together. The earth will be repositioned, and we must prepare ourselves."

It was a quiet ride the rest of the way home. We just watched the stars shoot across the sky. The odd thing was they were headed in the same direction. It was late in the evening when I arrived home. Everyone was still asleep Eric and I were tired and just crashed wherever we dropped our bags.

The next morning, we awakened to the smell of bacon and a sweet little girl staring at us with a plate of food.

"Hungry, big brothers?"

Her smile lit up the room.

"Of course, little sister, of course."

We freshened up and joined everyone at the breakfast table. Mom and dad joined us later. Becca had showed us how much of a big girl she was being by fixing breakfast for everyone.

My parents welcomed Eric and asked how things were with him. They would like to get to know him more. Eric said that would be nice. He told us to finish up with breakfast he had some work for us to do. Becca also wanted to spend time with us she says she had so much to tell us.

Mom told us about the ride home and how strange it was. Both explained how the night was just too eerie, wild animals were running across the road like something was chasing them.

Becca's fever was getting worse. Dad also said he thought he saw animal but didn't know if it was a coyote or a wolf. Either way he didn't care they got back just in time to get Becca to the emergency room. Turns out she had a mild fever and needs some rest. Dad rubbed the top of her head until she laughed. After breakfast we helped dad in the garage for a while.

You would think by living in a small town with all the craziness going on it would be a ghost town by now. But as I looked around, observing my neighbors. Everyone seemed happy, children played in the street.

People were just going about their daily routines; I guess no one can live in fear for the rest of their lives. Just take it one day at a time, however there are some of us that are not so lucky.

I needed to meet up with Elsha I really needed to see her. I got a hold of her and Tony and asked them to meet us at the library. I didn't want to be gone long because I also wanted to spend time with Becca.

Once at the library Elsha had that look in her eyes again. The one she gives me when she has to know what's going on. I knew she was angry with me and Tony didn't really care as much but he was glad to see us.

"Nice to have both of you back here with us bro."

Eric laughed.

Eric slightly punched Tony in his arm.

"Good to see you again to if you want to lose again during our next game I don't mind."

"Hey that was a tie you haven't beat me yet."

I stepped in between them both.

"Alright, alright you two knock it off."

Elsha agreed she stated we had something to catch up on. And she wanted to know if the strange man on the reservation was ever found.

Yep that's my girl always persistent, always wanting answers. She is the niece of a cop. We sat down at the end of the round table in the back of the library. I explained to Elsha that the man was caught. Then she inquired about Nai'okah I told her that she was fine.

Elsha didn't buy it she was way too smart for that. I knew she had much to ask and much to say and just as I knew she would Elsha didn't waste any time.

"Come on you guys I don't have much time. While my dad is out of town again my uncle has me on a tight curfew right now. I need to know what happened after we left the reservation."

Before I could respond Eric questioned her.

"Why do you want to know so much?"

Uh oh, the look she just gave Eric was not a good one.

"When I run into a strange man that sniffs me like he is some kind of a blood hound then suddenly disappears that's why I want to know so much."

Before this got ugly, I calmed Elsha for a moment.

"Look guys there is so much going on right now let's not fight."

I explained how things did get a little scary, but everyone is okay. I told Elsha not to worry they guy was caught and Nai'okah was fine. Whether she believed me or not I did not care. I had too much on my mind right now and was not in the mood for arguments.

Eric's eyes glared at me while I spoke, I glared back letting him know I had things under control. Elsha shared her story about keeping the children calmed when strange noises were coming from the outside.

Tony also confirmed it; although they both were suspicious, they knew well enough in their minds what was going on. They also mentioned how Professor Flynn talked about returning to the reservation to do research. Then she asked about Veronica Banks and wondered if I had heard from her as well.

I told Elsha that I haven't checked any of my messages, but she also asked about Ms. Creed. Elsha talked about how determined she was to find out what was happening. I didn't want to tell Elsha how right she was about Ms. Creed having a daughter.

Before she could even ask, I changed the subject, then my cell rang. I asked everyone to give me a few minutes while I took the call. Elsha continued talking. It was my mom reminding me not to be out late, Becca wanted to spend time with me.

She was such a sweet little girl, so young and very brave I know she wants to talk. I too I just wanted to talk about something else for a while but what was there to talk about with our town under curfew, people are still disappearing.

It's as if a serious purge is destroying our town. This place was once a happy place; I just wish things would return to normal.

I'm happy I have my brother, family and my friends, a lot have happened in the past few days. Getting to know by brother, I now have a little sister, finding out that I have a remarkable gift that shocked me. I guess when you are in a life or death situation anything is possible when you are in survivor mode.

I heard laughing going on, so I decided to rejoin the group. Tony and Eric were having an arm-wrestling match.

These two are so competitive one always trying to outdo the other. Elsha just shook her head at both of them. Laughter is something I wanted to hear; we all sat down and talked about the fun we had on the reservation.

Tony thought it was cool how Eric and I danced along side of each other. I had no idea that was going to happen. My mind also reflected on the night I met Nai'okah she was so scared and had no Idea what she was up against.

She reached out for help and there was not much I could do; I guess the look on face raised concerns.

"Hey bro are lost in space again?"

Tony thought it was cool how Eric and I danced along side of each other. I had no idea that was going to happen. My mind also reflected on the night I met Nai'okah she was so scared and had no Idea what she was up against. She reached out for help and there was not much I could do; I guess the look on face raised concerns.

"Hey bro, you lost in space again?"

Tony asked.

"I'm fine, just glad to hear laughter for once. There's nothing like having a good time with friends."

Eric agreed, he said he kept to himself on the reservation because not too many of the kids there spoke to him. He said only the day I arrived and then people started talking. Saying they wondered how he could be in two places at once. Tony agreed he said it shocked it to see that I had a twin brother. Elsha also commented asking Eric if he had the same dreams as I did. Because twins sometimes share thoughts and dreams, they are often known to finish each other's sentences.

Eric looked at me and his thoughts were in my head. He spoke with his eyes and asking me was Elsha always this way.

I replied

"Yes".

Not trying to be so obvious, I played it cool. This was a little awkward but anything to keep her from knowing too much. But this is Elsha she has quite the gift of getting the answers she wants.

Then a strange thing happened, Eric stared at Elsha long and hard. She was even puzzled; it was as if he saw something deep within her. He looked at me then walked out.

"Did I say something wrong?"

I didn't know what to say. But Elsha didn't care. We continued talking for a while; she asked about Becca again and said she would like to pick her up to bring her to the horse ranch. I said she would like that a lot. Then it was time for me to leave, but not before an odd feeling came over me. With shaky hands and sweaty palms, I knew this feeling. It was an anxiety attack almost.

I could feel someone trying to reach out to me. Elsha knew me all too well.

"Kyle you've got that long stare again. What is going on? Kyle please say something!"

I spaced out for a moment, and then I came to myself again. Tony and Elsha knew something was wrong. I looked at them both for a moment.

"I've gotta go."

Elsha grabbed my arm, and Tony put his hand on my shoulder.

"Dude, you are not leaving, what just happened?"

I apologized to them both, I know they were concerned. I hate when this happens, but someone is trying to reach me, but I don't know who. I explained to my friends how grateful I was to have them. They have been with me since the beginning; I knew they deserved an explanation. But I didn't have an answer there was defiantly another shift in the balance. I wonder if Eric felt it as well.

I tried my best to keep my composure, but the force was just too strong. Eric had returned and rushed to my side. I fell to the floor; something in my eyes must have frightened Elsha. She backed away from me.

"What is wrong with him, I don't like seeing him like this. Come on let's take him to my house."

I raised my hand.

"No." I'm okay just another odd feeling that came over me. Trust me I'm okay."

Chapter Five

NIGHT CRIES

Tony laughed a little he said most people have normal friends; I have friends with special gifts. I know he was trying to change things up a bit. I know everyone was curious and wanted to know more, but I assured them when I get my thoughts together I would.

Elsha asked if I cared to share with her, I told her I'd rather not. Just then she received a call phone rang and she walked away. It was probably her dad or uncle checking up on her. The look on Eric's face told me he felt it to.

She mentioned she is at the library with friends. They must have asked if I were there the way she looked at me. She handed me her phone.

"Here my dad wants to talk to you."

I didn't know what to say, but I didn't want to keep the good doctor waiting.

"Hello Dr. Morgan, sir."

I was a nervous wreck. I wondered why he asked to speak with me.

"Kyle, hello I only have a few minutes to talk. I'm in Rocky Point and I was on my back home when I received a phone call from one of the local townspeople to say there was a little girl suffering from terrible nightmares."

I just had to ask him about his concerns.

"Excuse me Dr. Morgan what does any of this have to do with me?"

Dr. Morgan continued.......

"I'm getting to that, Kyle just listen. When I arrived at the home, I found a little girl in a deep sleep calling out your name. She kept asking for you to come help her, now I don't know what to make of this, but I was hoping you could tell me."

I paused for a moment, I didn't know what to do or if I could do anything at this point. I had to get myself in a place where I could really focus. I needed to know who the little girl was. He said the daughter of a local teacher named Ms. Creed.

I asked him if Ms. Creed has arrived yet, she should have been there by now. Perhaps that was the urgency I was feeling.

"Dr. Morgan has her mother arrived yet?"

His response was very quick.

"No there was a flight delay but he she should be here soon. Kyle is this little girl in danger, and if so, what can I do to help?"

I gave him my number and told him to call me once her mother arrived. Dr. Morgan said there had been several other cases and he had no idea how to help the children. I told him there was nothing he could do but consult the elders in the area. Before he hung up, he said the necklace the little girl wore was very unique. I responded by saying.

"Is it glowing?"

Dr. Morgan said he'd never seen anything like this one before, I asked him what he meant, He said in the past he noticed others wearing these silver stones but the one this little girl is wearing sparkled like a cosmic galaxy of stars.

I asked him how long he could stay with her he said he would for a little while before heading back home.

I handed the phone back to Elsha, she told her dad to be safe, but she questioned me on that.

"Kyle is my dad in danger?"

I just looked at her speechless she asked me again.

"Kyle is my father in danger? Please tell me?"

Eric looked over at me; Tony looked nervous fumbling his thumbs. My gut told me that he was, so I told her.

"We all are in danger; ever since I've discovered who I was I'm afraid this will not stop. Native blood or not we all are in danger."

I started to walk out of the library, Elsha said we all are affected by the same things, but something out there wants more than just native blood it wants war. I stopped in my tracks, as I turned to face her, I looked deep within her eyes anger burned inside me.

"You are right it has been waging war for centuries, it has thirsted after our blood, killed off our people by hunting them down like cattle. Attacking them in dreams, this nightmare is not going to end until this until dark entity is destroyed."

I must have had that look again, Elsha was tough but whatever reflection she saw in my eyes must have startled her. Tony and Eric asked me to calm down a little; everyone was on edge I apologized to Elsha for letting my emotions get the best of me. She said she was used to it. It told her I would keep in touch I needed to get home to spend time with Becca.

Elsha said she also needed to get home before her uncle the Chief of Police calls her. Eric and I left the library; I asked him if he had sensed something earlier and he said he did. I told him how I felt someone was in trouble. On the way home, we talked about many things including our parents.

He said he was very grateful that Benjamin cared enough to tell us the truth about our parents. My mind reflected on the dream of the woman giving birth to twin boys.

They were separated and hidden from their father, I somehow know this, and Le'liana was the mother so Li'wanu was the father. The Elders hid the boys, so he couldn't find them. We are his descendants. The more I thought about this the more real it became. My thoughts must have been loud enough for Eric to hear. He said he felt there was something to us but never like this.

Once we arrived home, mom was just finishing dinner. She said Becca was waiting upstairs, and how she had a few errands to run. She said dad would be home later and if we were to leave the house we needed to be back before dark.

I could hear Becca running down the stairs to greet us.

"Big Brothers, big brothers it's about time."

She gave each of us a hug and said that she really needed to talk. I didn't feel like discussing much, I just wanted her to enjoy being a kid. I suggested we go to a park or go watch a movie. Eric thought some fresh air would do Becca some good. But I thought about the park issue, not sure if she was ready to go to the park since that is where her parents died. But Becca has proven to be a strong brave little girl.

Eric and I decided to let Becca choose what she wanted to do. And she suggested and Ice cream parlor.

We headed out to The Parlor Palace it was one of the local hang out places for kids, and they had the best ice cream in town. I remember my parents bringing me here when I was a kid and the owner Mr. Salvador Vitaly would come out and rub me on top of my head.

He was a funny guy; his family migrated here from Italy years ago, so they decided to keep the family tradition going by opening up the ice cream parlor. He spoke with a thick Italian accent and always smiled when he greeted people.

We approached the counter to place our order, when Mr. Vitaly greeted us.

"Buon giorno, my friend it's good to see you alive and well. What can I get for you today?"

I smiled and told I would have my usual strawberry banana shake, Becca ordered a banana split and when he got to Eric, he paused. He looked at me, then at Eric. He started speaking Italian and shaking his head.

"I never knew you had a twin brother, what a resemblance. Are you trying to give an old guy a heart attack I thought I was seeing double?"

Laughing at him I told him no, I introduced Eric and Becca and told him it was a long story. He said he would love to hear it sometime. Then he took Eric's order and said it was on the house. Mr. Vitaly was a very generous man.

He told us to find a table and he would bring our desserts. I told him he didn't have to, but he said it would be his pleasure to serve us. We found a nice quiet booth with a beautiful view of the mountain. When Mr. Vitaly brought our desserts Becca's eyes widened. Mr. Vitaly placed a huge ice cream sundae in front of her. Becca thanks him and smiled.

"Gracias, Señor."

Mr. Vitaly placed his hand on his chest and smiled back at Becca.

"Grazie, enjoy and please take your time."

Before he left our table, he stared Eric one more time. He shook his head and spoke in Italian while walking away from us. We all just laughed, as we started to enjoy our ice cream, I asked Becca how she was doing. She said she was doing okay, and how she said she felt safe because she knows her parents are watching over her and she has two strong big brothers to take care of her.

No wonder my mom spoils her, for one she got a daughter now and she gets to do girlie things with her. I will never forget the night I found her in the house; she was so scared the look in her face was frightening. I enjoyed watching her have fun; she needs it I wish we didn't have to face such an evil that has all of us on alert.

I just wanted to feel normal again this gift I have is a blessing and a curse to me. I thought about Ms. Creed's daughter Nai'Jae. She needed my help again; I tried to focus on spending time with my brother and little sister, so I tried shaking it off.

Eric glared at me to get my attention; he must have sensed my concern.

"Hey brother focus our little sister is trying to tell a story here."

I looked at them both and apologized. Becca said it was okay, she noticed how I stared off for a moment. We laughed and talked more for a while; Eric told jokes to make Becca laugh. He reminded me of Tony and how silly he acts sometimes.

Becca really enjoyed herself, especially when she decorated Eric's nose with whipped cream. I even mentioned to Becca if she would like to visit Elsha at her horse ranch and she said she would like that a lot. I told her how much Elsha wanted to spend time with her, Becca said she would like that a lot.

She looked at me and said it was nice to have me back at home, ever since that night she left the reservation she was scared for both of us. Becca said she had visions of a great war coming, where people from distant places would gather under a great moon to prepare for battle. She said it would take place where the great mountain meets the sky. Becca shared more of her dreams with us, and Eric and I just looked at each other.

Eric asked her if he could tell us more, but she couldn't, she said her fever was high and she said Helen was by her bed side. I didn't expect Becca to start calling her mom yet, but she told us how she stayed in the room with her until she was better. There was one time she screamed out my name because she dreamed, I was in a fight with a dark entity. I told Becca she didn't have to talk about it anymore, but she said she needed to. She turned her head looking toward the mountain.

"Someone is in trouble and needs our help, one is locked in and the other crying out for your big brother. I too have felt her, and she is just as strong as me. When one entity is destroyed another one more strong and powerful than the other comes."

Then Becca turned and looked at me, staring into my eyes. Just as she did it was as if a cloud had covered the sun and the sky darkened. Becca said she has been hearing the cries of many people that are tormented by the night. She tries to block them out but one voice she hears she has a strong connected to.

Eric asked her if she could give details of the voice if she could tell who the person was.

Becca said she didn't know but there was a way to find out. It was time to head home and Becca said she would show us what she meant. I asked her if it was dangerous and she said more than what we have already been faced with. Her bravery was beyond measure.

I didn't want to go playing around with Pandora's Box. But it seems already Pandora's Box chose to play with me. By the time we arrived home, Elsha dad had called and said the young girl's mother had arrived. He had no idea that we all had the same thing in common and we knew each other.

Ms. Creed was very frantic, and Becca said there was not time to waist. I asked how Nai'Jae was doing and there was no change, somehow, she slipped into a deep sleep and could not be wakened.

I asked to speak with Ms Creed and Dr. Morgan placed her on the phone.

"Kyle, what can we do, my baby needs help! Tribal Elders should be arriving any minute I don't want to lose my baby!"

I told her anything was possible at this point and that she should try and stay calm. A cloud of distress began to circle me. I felt Ms. Creeds pain, something wanted Nai'Jae and I knew how badly. I helped her before and I knew I could do it again but this time I was going to have help. Becca seemed to be willing to help but this was too dangerous.

It was at least a four-hour drive to get to them mom would not like that too much. The only thing I could do was to pray and ask the great spirits to watch over her.

Dr. Morgan said he would stay with Ms. Creed and keep an eye on her daughter. I told him I would keep in touch.

Becca said she wanted to help, I told her to just pray and things would get better. By the look on her I knew she didn't believe me. But I needed her to believe, for NaiJae's sake. Eric thought perhaps it would be best for us to go to Rocky Point.

"Nai'Okah is locked in and can't wake up now Ms. Creed's daughter, whose next? Come on brother I know you feel it to. Something is going on in the spirit world that is affecting the living. When we were at the hospital standing around Nai'Okah's body I felt that she is there for a reason. What if the same thing is happing to Nai'Jae?"

I had to process this for a minute, he was right, but we can't go to the rescue of everyone this happens to. Becca came and stood by my side.

"Big brother I know you are worried, I'm scared for them to. Even though we all have to face our destiny they need our help."

Becca was right; she told me how her mother used to practice sacred prayers in their home. She said her mother would light candles and stay locked in her room for days. Her father would tell her stories about strange events taking place in their home before she was born.

Her mother would pray for wandering souls trapped between worlds. One night her mother couldn't sleep. She talked about how her room got very cold one night and when she sat up in her bed. A ghostly shadow of a little girl was in her room. She said it was a soul that was trapped so her mother helped her to cross over.

I asked her how her mother helped the souls to cross over, Becca said she never questioned her mom about it until a week before she died. Her mother told her that there will come a time she is going to have to use her gifts to help those in need. Not all spirits are bad, but there are some that are evil.

I rubbed my arm as a reminder. It was still a little dangerous, so I suggested we stayed home until mom and dad returned.

Chapter Six

TRANSITIONS

However, Eric felt we should go, and I didn't want Becca to go either. She was so strong for her age. Eric talked about how quickly things can change, earlier we were having fun laughing and talking. Now we are talking about facing danger again. We have so much to do, and it seems not enough time to do it. Becca kept asking to go to Rocky Point and I kept saying no.

Eric said perhaps we should call Uncle Benjamin, but I really didn't feel like talking to anyone at this point.

We all started to argue amongst ourselves about what to do, and where and when to go. Rocky Point is not a safe place to go right now. We are still under curfew until further notice. Besides I don't think that mom and dad would allow us to take Becca with us.

This would require strong minds coming together to save a young girl. But what if Eric is right about Nai'Jae being chosen, he looked at me with his eyes glaring.

"I want to be wrong, but what if we are being tested again? After what happened on the reservation when we were looking for Nai'Okah."

I shook my head at him. Becca wanted to know what he meant.

"What do you mean? What happened to Nai'Okah? She was the missing girl, right?"

There was no keeping this from her at all.

"I knew it, I told you something bad was going to happen, she's the one I've been seeing her in my dreams. She's very pretty and she warns me telling me how to get to safety." We've got to help her."

There were a few things I needed to explain to Becca first. Although it appears Nai'Okah is helping her in her dreams, there was another little girl who has fallen in to a deep sleep. Eric spoke what I had been thinking we wouldn't tell Becca about Ms. Creed's daughter, but we would see what she could discern. I asked Becca to clear her mind and her thoughts to see if there were any others that may have helped her.

Eric had a different opinion about this. Becca would also be tracked this way and that she was too young. I told him it doesn't matter we all have been tracked in some way or another besides I know how strong she is. Eric cautioned me not to have her do it.

Although Becca wanted to participate, she always wanted to be like her mother to help those who needed help. She looked at Eric and told him that she would be fine; Eric had never seen the look Becca gets when she uses her gifts. Her eyes grow wide and color darkens, her dead stare could startle anyone.

I asked Eric and Becca to give me a moment; I went up to my room to relax for a moment. My head was filled with so much stuff I needed a break. Eric said he would take Becca outside for a while to play baseball. She enjoyed the sport and wanted to play on a real team one day.

I lay down on my bed for a while to clear my mind. Although it was hard to focus when so much was going on around me. Finding out who I was, I feel like I have a real family now. I don't want to lose any of them. I will protect Becca to the far ends of the earth. I whispered the words in my head.

"Far ends of the earth, Hmmmm, I know that means something."

In my dreams I remembered seeing a vision of four men standing with their backs opposite of each other. Each praying towards the direction they stood in, somehow back then I knew those prayers was prayed to protect the future generations of tribes. Their stones glowed brightly around their necks, I can almost see them. These sacred men are the keepers of the four corners I can sense them, they are very strong.

The more I thought about them the more I could see them; they are as ancient giants glistening in white. They stood tall and strong watching the sky above, and the sky below. Galaxies of stars surrounded them. I could also see two tall white pillars with a beautiful waterfall sparkling flowing out of nowhere, it had no beginning, but I could see where it flowed from.

I'm not sure why I was having this vision. But it must be for a good reason; there was no sun however the stars were bright enough to cast an illuminating light. There was no sound either, just a mild humming noise. It wasn't like anything I saw when I met my real parents. But this place was real, very real just opposite of our world.

I felt myself drawn to them, the power that I felt so very overwhelming, I couldn't get close to them but was I was only allowed to come so far. As I walked toward them, I looked down to see nothing but sky and stars beneath me.

Then a stream of water separated me from getting close to the men. With their arms folded and their staffs glowing bright, they spoke simultaneously but their lips didn't move.

"The stars are aligning young warrior, time draws near, and many are traveling from distant places, what is your request."

Lost in confusion, I replied.

"Request, I have no request. What does all of this mean?"

"Only those that travel this far, come seeking the knowledge of their great ancestors of long ago. For generations we have watched over the corners of the earth and have seen life, death and destruction of our people. We watch over the chosen ones guiding them to safety. Again young warrior, your mind may not comprehend what the heart speaks, clear your thoughts and combine your mind with the heavens and let it speak to you."

I did as they suggested, clearing my mind, I focused on my heart beat, it sounded like a beating drum, but in slow reps. A soft wind cooled my skin, I could hear a faint voice, but I couldn't make out who it was. The sound of the water sounded like ancient prayers, my eyes beheld, warriors riding on the wings of eagles.

The faint voice was getting stronger; I could see people crossing over in a light that illuminated from the heavens above, some descended while others ascended. I'm not sure what was happening here, but I allowed myself to be drawn deeper into it.

The great elders stood aiming their staffs each in the direction they were faced. Large beams of lights flew out of them like shooting stars.

I know I have seen this before, I wanted to move closer to them, but the water prevented me. I needed to know more about the chosen ones, so I decided to clear my mind and allow the heavens to speak to me. I could see and hear many things. I focused my mind to get more of an understanding, so I turned to them once again.

"Why do some of the chosen fall into a deep sleep? What happens to them?"

Budging not one time, the ancient ones explained.

"When destiny calls it can pull you into an unfamiliar direction. The gifts that lie within are much stronger in the environment from which they came. Only destiny knows their fate, some return others do not."

I didn't like the way this conversation was going.

"What happens to them, please tell me."

"They take their place among the heavens, placed among the stars, just as we remain so will they."

I thought this was a choice to protect the generations. They must have read my mind.

"All of us have a choice young warrior, but some of us can't change what we are destined for. Just as you are able to communicate with us, we can't change that, your connection to this world is a very strong one. But not even you know how long that will be."

Then my eyes opened to find Becca and Eric standing over me. Eric nudged me in my side.

"Hey brother naps over it's time for dinner."

"Dinner, how long was I sleep? Are mom and dad back already?"

Becca and Eric said I wasn't sleep long however they did state how loud I was snoring. They both made jokes as we headed downstairs. Mom was setting the table and asked if everyone had washed up.

She called for Becca to help her in the kitchen. Dad finishing up in the garage putting away boxes, the sound my stomach made could wake the dead it was so loud. This would be the first time Eric would get to know them, I'm glad he is here all I wanted to do was focus on my family enjoy a wonderful dinner. I also wanted to see what my parents have been up to.

Mom said she wants to enroll Becca into a dance class like ballet or something, but she is more focused on playing sports. Dinner talk was actually quite nice, both my parents said they never knew I had a twin and if they had known they would have raised both of us together. Mom was glad she had a daughter now they asked Eric how long he planned on staying on the reservation. He said he didn't know, dad said that it would stir up some people doing double takes if it hasn't happened already.

Becca, Erica just laughed; we told them about Mr. Vitaly at the Ice cream parlor seeing double. Dad and mom laughed hard, it was good to have laughter, but I couldn't help but feel a little depression with other things on my mind. A kick under the table from Becca kind of helped me to keep focus. After dinner mom prepared the spare bedroom for Eric, to sleep in, dad also asked Eric about life on the reservation.

He didn't go in too much detail he just said how good it felt to getaway. Both dad and mom talked about how much they enjoyed being there. We laughed and talked more, Dad asked if I had any plans, I told him that I would meet up with Elsha and Tony later.

Speaking of which, I really missed her and wanted to talk to her. Mom asked if I had heard from her, she mentioned how busy her dad has been traveling back and forth. With all of the weird things happening around town she wondered if he would even get a break.

Well after dinner mom and Becca cleared the table, while Kyle and I washed the dishes. I received a call from Dr. Morgan stating that Nai'jae's condition had not changed they were going to move her to the local hospital there. Ms. Creed was very worried, Chief Spearhorn was due to arrive soon.

My heart sank, but I also felt that she would be okay. When destiny chooses you age limits don't matter, we all have road we travel leading in many directions. Sometimes we never know where we will end up.

After cleaning the kitchen, I decided to go to my room for awhile, I wanted to call and talk to Elsha but I wanted to check my emails first.

Wow there were so many, I went through all two hundred of them and deleted the unwanted junk and spam mail. Later I found my eyes getting heavy, I tried to stay awake, but sleep was starting to get the best of me.

Until a quick buzz from my phone alerted me. It was a text message from Elsha asking if I was awake.

I replied *"yes"* back to her, she responded with *"need to talk right away"*. I called Elsha and of course she was her usual self.

I called her asking what the emergency was; she told me how much she was worried about her dad. She said she must have called him at the wrong time. I asked her what she meant by that, she replied.

"When my father answered, he was a little distressed, he sounded very tired and I told him to get some rest and he refused. He told me he was very busy and that I was to go to my uncles and stay there until he returned."

I laughed a little and just assured her that he was dealing with a lot of patients and was probably tired. I yawned trying to tell her just as he was tired so was I. But Elsha had more to say.

"Look Kyle I know my dad is busy, but I feel he brushed me off, I think my dad has a girlfriend."

Now I really laughed.

"What? So, what if he does? He's a single guy."

Elsha was getting a little agitated.

"Come on Kyle I'm serious and I believe it is with someone we both know."

Now I was even more curious, so I asked.

"Who do you think this person is Elsha?"

With a deep sigh and a slow response, she uttered.

"Ms. Creed."

Elsha was serious and I thought to myself well Ms. Creed is a very beautiful woman. And besides who could blame the man.

"So what makes you think your dad is seeing Ms. Creed."

She didn't like my sarcasm as much, but this issue seemed to bother her.

"Well he visits Rocky Point a lot and lately I found out that Ms. Creed does to. I know her parents live there as well. But I just got this gut feeling there is more to this story."

I told Elsha how one day she would make a great detective, and I didn't want to spend time talking about it.

"Well Elsha he is entitled to have a life you know, and besides don't you think he deserves to be happy?"

She began to get defensive stating how close she is to her dad and his work keeps him away, at first, I didn't read between the lines then I caught on. When Elsha's parents split up she wanted to stay with her dad, while her mom traveled the world. But looking at her situation a little closer she was alone. No wonder she spends her time keeping busy. I couldn't help but wonder if she feared being alone.

She kept rambling on about her dad and Ms. Creed, so I asked her if she had proof. She said she didn't need proof she just knew. She talked about how her open her dad is with her, but she also felt that his work keeps him away from having a private life. Then she got on one of her tangents about Ms. Creed again.

"Well since she is a woman of many secrets, then he is a man with a secret."

I just sighed and rolled my eyes.

"Elsha don't go there again, you act as if no one can have a life accept you, I have a lot of respect for Ms. Creed and you should to, besides what did she ever do to you anyway."

I was really trying to control my emotions, but this girl sometimes likes to push buttons.

"Look Kyle all I'm saying is what I feel, don't get so freaking defensive! He's down there because of her and I know it!"

Elsha had no clue what was happening, but she did have connections, so I had to be careful not to disclose too much information. As we argued back and forth, I explained I knew how important her dad is to her and how hard it must be to want your parents around when they are not there.

But in his line of work he is also needed by other people and he offers his assistance when and where ever he is needed.

I can understand her selfishness though, her dad is gone a lot, her mom sails the world with her rich husband.

No wonder Elsha feels the way she does. She kept rambling on about Ms. Creed but Elsha also had no idea what Ms. Creed was faced with. Nai'Jae's life was in danger. Elsha kept on talking about how scared she was of her father being in Rocky Point; every time he goes there someone dies.

"What could be more important there, he was on his way home and then he went back?"

I tried to calm her a bit.

"Elsha he is there helping out, just let him do his job and then he will return home."

Then she questioned me.

"Helping out whom? What do you know that you are not telling me? What could be more important than me?"

Oh boy here we go again; No matter how I tried to explain things to her she just kept going.

"Elsha please understand, with everything that is happening no one is safe, but there are those that are strong and those that are weak. And they need help; your father is a strong man let him do his job."

My native instincts began to kick in. Sounds and images flooded my brain, my breathing increased a little. I tried to calm myself, but I felt something shift inside me. Elsha doesn't know what it was like for me as a frightened little kid. I could only imagine what Ms. Creeds daughter was going through. Then what I knew and what Elsha didn't almost slipped out.

"Besides it's more than just Ms. Creed it's her…."

I couldn't go on. Elsha asked if it was her parents, I remained quiet.

"Kyle, are you there? Kyle, please answer me!"

No more keeping secrets I tell myself, sooner or later she is going to find out. I told her I would come see her tomorrow, since she promised Becca a horse ride. I would tell her then. I was too tired to say anything else.

Elsha agreed, I told her to get some rest and that we would meet her at her house tomorrow. Before going to bed I checked in on Eric to say goodnight. He was sitting on the floor Indian style with his feet together and arms crossed. Whatever he was doing I didn't want to disturb him, so I turned to walk out of his room.

"Don't leave brother, please come join me."

Chapter Seven

SILENT PRAYERS

Sitting down on the floor next to him I asked what was he doing?

"I'm praying while listening to the voices of nature. I saw Chief Spearhorn do this once when I also interrupted him. He says this is the way of our people to listen to nature speaking and hear what she has to say."

He told me to clear my mind and slow my breathing, to only meditate on the good things. Listen to the voice speak and hear what troubles her. I don't know how long we sat in meditation, I found myself in a place of darkness once again. Standing on a high mountain I watched darkness cover the land devouring everything in its path.

Nothing could escape it not even the animals. The earth rumbles as the sound of thunder. Then to my left I saw hundreds of men and women walking together side by side. And there rose up a great moon, full and bright light silver, each of them wore colors of their tribe bearing symbols on their face and arms. They were led by a great white buffalo, heading in the direction of the darkness.

They met in the middle of an open valley where even darker images began to emerge into men. Sounds of war drums were carried in the wind. The white buffalo stood and did not move, huge eagles flew high above, and their eyes glowing like diamonds. Truly this is the sign of the Great War, I kneeled and prayed for the people and the land, but the more I prayed, evil was against me. A disruption in the atmosphere shook like an earthquake, wolves transformed in to great beast, wearing the night as skin.

The only thing visible was their red glowing eyes. Then there was silence, no one moved, no one spoke. Each one of them standing, waiting on the other to move. Then a sound from above sounded like it was cracking open, whatever it was it was huge and coming fast, I couldn't tell who or what it was. This must be another vision of what is to come; I have had many dreams of natives from different tribes gathering under the rock where the earth meets the sky.

There have been many stories told about devils' tower, but what is so significant about this place. I know there are others out there like me. Sometimes I can feel their prayers of strength. As I stood, staring overlooking the valley it was as if time had stood still, there was no movement from either side of the plain. I wondered what they were waiting for; I could Eric calling out to me.

"Brother, hey, wake up we got to get going."

I could feel him nudging my side. My stiff body hurt to move. I must have fallen asleep on the floor. The last thing I remember was talking to Eric, meditating then him waking me up. He asked me if I cared to share my dream. I told him only if he shared his first, Eric began by telling me what he saw in his dreams. He said the sky was dark and full of stars.

There was sadness everywhere; he said he saw burial grounds everywhere. He said he watched in horror as shifters claimed more victims. Death was all around him. Those that were killed he saw white lights leaving their bodies. He said he knew what it meant but then his countenance changed. I asked him why he looked so grim in the face.

"You saw something else didn't you, what else did you see?"

Eric sat up down on his bed, I've never seen this look on his face before. Then he shared more of this dream.

"When I was younger, I was told many stories about trackers, last night I dreamed of more people turning against their own kind just to save their own lives. There was a great gathering under a full moon. It looked like a war was getting ready to happen."

Then he just stared at me, asking me if I was afraid to die, I told I didn't know. I shared my dream with him and we both knew what was coming. We knew we would have to leave soon to meet up with the others. The problem was how you tell your parents you're going away on a trip that you may never return from. Something is coming but it is bigger than what we think.

People are still dying I dreaded to even watch the news. After breakfast we headed over to Elsha's house and took Becca with us. Mom is so protective of her that she drilled me and Eric before we left. But not before she surprised Becca with some riding gear. Mom was all about safety.

"Please make sure you keep an eye on her and don't let her fall."

Mom was serious. I told her there was nothing to worry about; I would make sure she stayed safe. Becca was excited to ride horses with Elsha she couldn't wait until we arrived

I remember my first trip out here, so beautiful and peaceful. Then I remembered when we were trapped in the cave seeing that huge stone wall with the sacred symbols, I knew it was the tomb of the Liwanu.

I also know the dark-skinned man with the crystal blue eyes is the guardian.

Eric had never been here before either, he admired the country side. The rolling hills and mountains made everything so beautiful. Watching the tall trees sway in the wind was like watching a dancer gracefully dancing.

Becca was so excited, I tried to keep my focus and think positive. Being back out here just made me shiver but I was also glad to see Elsha. As we approached the house Becca nearly leaped out of the back seat when she saw the horses.

Rodrigo and the others were helping gather them, Boomer and Tango were running around while Elsha was walking along side of her horse. We headed up the driveway toward everyone and Becca took off running calling out to Elsha. She gave her a big hug and told her she was glad to see again.

"Are you ready to go for a ride?

Becca was so excited. Her eyes were glowing. It pleased my heart to see her so happy to go riding. Elsha

"Yes, I'm ready to go but first I need to change into my riding gear hear Heather bought for me."

Elsha said she would take her inside and help her get ready while Rodrigo came to greet me and Eric.

"Ola amigos, **Cómo estás?"**

I gladly replied.

"Doing well Rodrigo, how are you?"

I mentioned to Eric that how has been a longtime friend of Elsha's family. I introduced Eric to him and we all talked while we waited for the girls to come outside.

"Wonderful my friend, it is very good to see you alive and well. We thought we almost lost you."

He was very sincere, he told us how the many strange things have been going on that night we were missing. He said people claimed to have seen wolves as big as bears up in the hills and at Rocky Point.

He referred to them as *El Noche Diablo*; Becca told me it meant the night devil or demon. It is funny how many cultures see the same thing only to give it a different name. For centuries different cultures have seen many strange sightings recording them in cave walls and rocks and stone.

This is also how they pass their stories down from generation to generation. Rodrigo stated that night all of the animal were going crazy. Many Natives came and offered prayers; he said he also prayed for protection. When he saw me on the back of Wind Star he thought I was dead, I had lost a lot of blood. Some were afraid the smell of my blood would attract wild animals so Rodrigo poured ammonia on the ground.

He stood back staring and me and Eric shaking his head. Before saying anything else the girls came outside. Both in their riding gear, ready to go horseback riding.

We greeted the girls and I told Becca how cute she looked. Elsha also looked nice; I mean her curvy body was fitting so tight into those pants I just couldn't take my eyes off her.

"Wow you look wonderful Elsha."

She just smiled at me and graciously replied.

"Thanks Kyle."

My heart skipped a beat as I watched her help Becca get familiar with the horses. Speaking of horses, I noticed Wind Star wasn't around. Rodrigo said that he was with Elsha's dad in Rocky Point. He talked about how fast he was and how he moved swift like the wind.

He says he remembers the day when Wind Star first arrived. He called him a mystery horse because no one knew where he came from. He also said there was something very strange about the horse like it was destined to be here and knew its purpose.

He talked more as he watched Elsha lead the horse that Becca was riding.

We all waved to Becca as she rode the horse while Elsha slowly led the horse around a few hay barrels. She was having so much fun; Elsha kept her pretty occupied which was a good thing.

He told me how he noticed my staring at her. He said Elsha was a very tough girl and strong. Eric joked about me staring at her, and we laughed. As Eric looked around, he admired the house and the property. Then he asked to see the cave. Rodrigo spoke before I could respond.

"No, no, no, señor you must not go there, too dangerous!"

I looked at Rodrigo and telling him the cave is sealed there is no danger. But he thought different. I knew there was evil there as well however Rodrigo was quite disturbed about it.

"Señors por favor, stay away there. There is an evil spirit roaming and I don't want you getting into trouble. Only members of the tribal council are allowed, but even the cave is too dangerous for them."

Eric said he just wanted to see it from the outside. I told him I wasn't sure about going back to it either however I wondered if Elsha had ever returned. I asked Rodrigo why he felt, and that evil dwelled there. Looking at me and Eric it is as if her knew or could tell something about us both.

He told us how he has worked on the ranch before Elsha was born. I know that sometimes when the moon is high and full something out there makes the horses go crazy. Animals can sense danger but, on some nights, not a sound. One-night lightning struck one of the posts and a few horses got out.

Rodrigo told us how spooked horses are very hard to catch especially if you don't have a faster horse. He immediately took a few men with him took off after the horses during the storm. He said that night reminded him the night Elsha and I went missing. We caught one horse and the other one was not so lucky, if fell into a ravine it appeared to have a breaking its leg. While we stood over the dying animal, we said a silent prayer.

Then he told us something strange happened. The lightning got so bad they had to seek shelter under a small cliff surrounded by trees. They always pack emergency camping gear on their horses just in case they need it. They watched as horse the lay in pain and they made no attempts to move it because of the storm. As they sought shelter in the tents, they covered it with branches to camouflage it. One of the men thought he saw something moving toward the horse.

Peeking out from his tent, Rodrigo said he saw a tall dark figure moving toward it slowly.

Lightning appeared to reveal it when it flashed. He and the others remained quiet and still, and no one moved. He said as a child he heard stories of el Noche diablo. Demons that roam the night taking form as natural men sometimes and beast to. He said never all his life he would have witnessed such a horrifying thing.

Taking his rosary from around his neck, they waited in the dark praying for morning to come. As the men began to pray Rodrigo placed his finger in front of his lips silencing them quickly. He told the men to not to say a word or light their lanterns. Radios and cell phones were to be turned off. He could tell how frightened they were so relied on their faith and strength to get them through the night.

Then as the storm seem to pass, the men did not hear any sounds coming from outside the tent. Then before they could move, they heard the sound of wolves howling, and growling. Fear gripped them as the dark shadow hovered above. It appeared to stretch out over them mild flashes from the lighting revealed it was there. Long claw like hands stretching from beyond the darkness moved around them.

No sound, just darkness. He said they slowed their breathing and sat paralyzed in fear. He said he remembered the sacred prayer taught to him by his grandmother. When evil spirits enter the world, they look for victims to consume. So, the prayer he prayed was to ask the Holy Father to shield them from danger. He prayed for everyone to be hidden from the cloak of darkness. To make them invisible so no one could be seen.

He also described the sounds they heard that night. He said it would drive anyone crazy. Growls and high pitch screams cause them men to put their hands over their ears. He said he felt it knew they were there, and it was trying to drive the men out. Rodrigo talked about how he encourages the men to keep it together he felt one of them was about to lose his mind. He placed his hand on his shoulder to calm him, but it was hard. In fear of him making a run for it, he covered his mouth cautioning him to be still.

Listening to this sent a wave of chills through me. He said that night was the longest night of his life. When they emerged from the tent at daybreak, they looked around and the horse was gone. The blood trails on the ground indicated wild animals took the horse.

Rodrigo encouraged us to stay away from the cave. He said he did not want anything to happen to us but looking at me and Eric he studied us with his eyes.

"There is something very mysterious about you two, whatever you boys are planning, I pray you use caution."

We just looked at each other. Becca and Elsha were approaching, Rodrigo met them.

"Hola, niña's, did you enjoy your ride?"

Chapter Eight

DISTRESS CALL

Becca smiled from ear to ear. She was so happy she told him how much she enjoyed connecting with the horses. Elsha asked Becca if she was hungry and she said yes. Elsha asked us to join us on the porch for lunch she had prepared. She was a very good decorator; the table was nicely decorated with a white table cloth with a coral trim. The placemats were made of bamboo and she had a beautiful array of sunflowers in a nice crystal vase.

The food looked very good, too bad Tony is missing out. Elsha had prepared fruit salad, finger sandwiches; and sparkling punch with bits of real fruit. And for dessert she made fresh cookies. I didn't know the girl had it in her.

"When did you become so festive?"

As she passed out the plates, she told us how she used to help her mom set the table while she prepared dinner when they had important guests coming over. She said her mother is an outstanding decorator and her mom taught her a lot. We sat down and had lunch and Becca told Elsha how much she enjoyed riding horses and thanked her. After all she didn't have to do any of this for us.

We all sat down and had a wonderful lunch. Elsha asked Eric if he cared to ride a horse, Becca said she would teach him how. We all laughed, and then Elsha asked if she could speak with me alone for a moment. Becca asked if she could go watch Rodrigo put horseshoes on the horses. Eric volunteered to take her. Elsha and I took a walk on a short trail behind her house. She wanted to pick up where we left off. I encouraged her to let it go.

Ms. Creed is dealing with a lot and Dr. Morgan is helping her. Elsha was afraid of being replaced and it was scaring her. She argued with me how that was not the case. But I insisted that perhaps her dad was tired of being alone.

She glared at me for a moment.

"You know something don't you?

I quickly responded to her

"I know plenty of things that you don't, I just choose not to tell you."

She immediately fired back.

"Look whatever you know keep it to yourself. I have my ways!"

This girl was just too much, always looking for trouble and when she finds it she has to prove a point.

"Elsha please let's not fight okay, you dad is on an important mission right now and I'm sure he will explain things to you when he comes home. I know your dad is important too but in his line of work there are people that depend on him and need him more."

Elsha was getting agitated with me I could tell. I had no problem confronting her with the truth. however, she was so stubborn.

"Kyle, I don't want to fight either, I'm just a little on edge lately. I know how important my dad is and how others need him. But I was getting a little curious I guess, perhaps my dad and Ms. Creed are really good friends. I almost forgot how she is dedicated to her work as well. But it still doesn't justify the phone calls and I know my dad."

I knew she was not going to let this go. Dr. Morgan was with Ms. Creed but not for what Elsha thinks. I told her not to worry too much about her dad again.

"Look Elsha I know how you want your dad to be here, but there is something I must tell you and I don't want you getting upset. But I need you to hear me out first."

She gave me a worrisome look, but I was confident enough to tell her the truth. I told her she was right about her dad and Ms. Creed but not for what she was thinking about.

Before she gave me more of a meaner look than she already had. I explained.

"Yes, your dad is in Rocky Point with Ms. Creed and before you start going off on a tangent let me explain."

Elsha relaxed herself, stepped away from me and told me to go on.

"There is a little girl in Rocky point and she is semi-conscious. The only way I can describe it is that she is in a deep sleep almost. Some people may call it locked in, but she has been chosen by the spirit guides. We don't know if she is going to be released or if, she will spend her eternity watching over the living.

Destiny has dealt her a hand that seems unfair, but we will just have to wait and see."

Elsha was not shocked at all. Although she knew about Ms. Creed's daughter, she was very concerned.

"I told you! Didn't I tell you? I knew she had a daughter, I knew it! But on the other hand, I felt sorry that Ms. Creeds daughter has to go through this terrifying ordeal."

Elsha's sympathy was very forgiving since I haven't heard much from her dad or Ms. Creed, I thought I would call to check in. But not before Tony called in a panic.

"Hello."

"Dude, where are you."

"I'm at Elsha's what's up?"

"Get to a television set now you've got to see this!"

His voice was so frantic. I told him to give me a few minutes to get inside the house. I asked him what was wrong he told me there was mass hysteria going on. By the time we approached the front of the house Eric and Becca met us. I told Tony I would call him later.

The looks on their faces told a chilling story and they also knew it as well.

"Brother, I feel weird; something is happening I just know it. Señor Rodrigo told me to keep safe and remember to say my prayers."

Eric suggested we should leave and take Becca home. Elsha asked if Rodrigo was around. Eric informed her that Rodrigo had to leave on an emergency. Something about a phone call he received that sent him and the others speeding out of the driveway.

She wondered what was happening herself. We quickly went inside and turned on the television.

Breaking news was everywhere, about wolf attacks and missing people most of the missing were children.

The news reporter said that there had been overwhelming 911calls of wolves being spotted in residential areas. Children missing from their beds, local Sherriff offices are baffled and have urged residence to be on high alert.

I sensed something in the air, and so did Eric, it was like a distress call or something. Someone was sending a message and we just received it.

Elsha went to call her dad, but not before her uncle Police Chief Morgan got a hold of her.

"Hi uncle what's up?"

"Elsha are you at home?"

"Yes, I'm here with Kyle, he brought his sister and brother over to ride horses."

"Listen to me, I need you to get to the house right away your aunt is there waiting on you I will explain the details later."

I could hear Elsha asking him why, and what was he planning. But whatever her uncle said to her didn't go so well.

"Why don't you just tell me? Did you talk to my dad?"

"Unfortunately, I didn't speak to your dad I have been trying to get a hold of him for several hours. Trust me in what I'm saying pack your things and get to my house."

After speaking with her uncle, she immediately called her dad, but he didn't answer.

"Dad it's me Elsha please call me back."

She looked at me with a worried look on face. I asked her what her uncle said to her and she said that she needed a ride to her aunt's house. Something was going on and she needed to find out. The news reported strange events were taking place almost simultaneously, missing people and gruesome discoveries sent shock waves through small towns. Gun sales were on the rise and people were fleeing their homes.

Eric suggested we take Becca home right away, but when I looked around, she was gone. How selfish of me to allow her to see such things on television. We called out to her and no answer. Elsha ran upstairs to check her room, where she found Becca staring out of the window.

She was in a deep stare Elsha called out to me to come upstairs. Eric followed behind. Elsha asked what was wrong with her and I told her I wasn't sure.

I gently called out to her.

"Becca, are you alright?"

She didn't move, and then Eric called out to her.

"Hey kiddo, we were worried about you, it's time to go home."

She didn't move, I could see her reflection in the window and her eyes were darkened, fixed on the woods. Elsha whispered to me.

"Kyle what's wrong with her, is she in some kind of trance? What is she looking at?"

There was no time to explain, I didn't want to interrupt her I didn't know what would happen, so I called out to her again.

"Becca, Becca."

She slowly turned her head towards us it was so creepy; I have never seen her like this before. She was like a zombie, she didn't even blink. Her eyes were so dark. She appeared to be driven by something as she walked toward us. I encouraged Elsha and Eric not to move or say anything whatever was happening out there is affecting her.

Perhaps he wouldn't have to wait long enough to find out.

Still looking straight ahead Becca grabbed my hand and immediately sat down on the floor. I encouraged Eric to do the same. Elsha stood back and watched asking what we were doing.

I told her not to move or speak. We sat in a circle watching her, something was taking place where ever she was, and we needed to join forces with her. Eric shivered as if a chill came over him, I felt it as well.

Heaviness came over me; I closed my eyes for a second. Becca uttered a few words in Spanish, I watched her eyes grow even wider and her breathing increased. Eric whispered to me telling me we should stop, I told him we must continue, she has no control over what she sees.

"Brother this is too dangerous for her, she is too young, and we should wake her."

I quickly replied.

"No! We can't we must continue there is no time."

Just as we don't have control, it comes for a reason and sometimes we have to embrace what we can't see and trust what we don't know. We needed to keep our thoughts clear. Then I heard a very faint voice speak through Becca, but it was not hers.

"Kyle, help me please help me they are everywhere."

I knew this voice it was Nai'jae, a strong energy force propelled us into a world unlike our own. Red and ash gray clouds hovered above us. Focusing on her voice I called out to her.

"Nai'jae, can you hear me?"

Faint cries were everywhere, whatever this place was it had to be what she was dreaming and experiencing. Although Becca didn't speak, she pointed to a place beyond the darkness, Eric removed his pouch from around his neck. Uttering a native prayer, white smoke arose from the ground like a thick dense fog. Eerie sounds were all around us I whispered to Eric.

"Keep your focus brother we are not alone in here."

Stepping into an even darker abyss, we saw the body of a young child laying in suspension, floating almost. Her hands were across her chest and she had scratch marks on her arms. Thick dark mist of fog circled her body. Blood dripped from her arms, and then there was no sound. Eric sprinkled crystal like dust on the ground; it crackled and sizzled as we walked. As we approached her something moved up from the ground, the smell of burnt flesh filled the air.

It was huge with long sharp teeth and claws then it spoke in a deep voice.

"You will not make it out of here alive, we are too many and you are too weak. She belongs to us now I have tasted her blood."

We stood our ground, the night moved as more eyes peered through the darkness. We knew we were in for a fight of our life, but we had to break the strong hold over Nai'Jae.

Chapter Nine

Dark Ghost

Eric said this kind of beast is a tracker. Standing face to face with the beast neither Eric nor I moved. Sensing shifters all around us, we were in her nightmare. I had battled one before and was not afraid to do it again. I motioned Eric to move forward toward the beast, its claws sharp as razors; we were neither intimated nor afraid. I did sense there was more on our side than against us. The beast let out a loud growl revealing its teeth.

Others surrounded Nai'Jae as we moved in closer. Then another ghostly figure appeared surrounding the beast, I couldn't tell if it was good or evil. An unfamiliar voice told me when to move. It was déjà vu all over again. Whoever or whatever this dark ghost was, was on our side. We needed to get Nai'Jae out of here if that beast tasted her blood she would surely turn.

I don't know what else was happening in this nightmare, but other voices started to call out to me for help. Eric told me to keep my focus, we had to act quickly. The dark ghost moved toward the shifter giving me time to grab Nai'Jae and get out of this nightmare. We needed a way of escape to get out and then I heard it.

"Kyle, this way, hurry, hurry!"

Moving through the dark abyss, we followed the voice. It spoke again.

"Hurray, you don't have much time!"

A light up ahead of us had to be the way out, the closer we got to the light, Nai'Jae's eyes began to move. She moaned, and softly spoke.

"Kyle, you came for me."

With Eric behind me and seconds from the bright light, she disappeared from my arms. As we passed through breaking the circle, we both gasped for air. Becca was shaking a little, but she was fine. Elsha asked if we were okay, she wanted to know what she just witnessed.

"Oh my gosh are you two alright! What happened?"

Eric still breathing heavy responded.

"You don't want to know."

Becca was slowly coming out of it. It took us a few minutes to get ourselves together. Elsha helped Becca on to her feet; she was still a little dizzy. Elsha escorted her to the couch and got her glass of water.

"Care to tell me what happened in there, should I be worried about you?"

Becca wiped the water from her mouth and told Elsha about her visions, and how sometimes she can't control what she sees. She said she felt someone was in trouble and saw heard voices of a little girl asking for help.

"Who was this little girl?"

Becca continued.

"I've never seen her before, but she had blood all over her and she was surrounded by darkness. I don't know how or why but I needed to help her. I'm sorry I walked away but I didn't want to scare anyone. Please don't be mad at me."

Elsha put her arms around Becca comforting her. She told her she was not mad just worried, Eric also comforted Becca to reassure her. Elsha still wanted answers.

"Will someone please tell me what else is going on here; I sat here in sheer panic watching your lifeless bodies."

I would explain but first I needed to call Ms. Creed I needed to know about Nai'Jae's condition. I also encouraged Elsha to try calling her dad again. Neither one of them answered. I just had to know if she was safe.

We spent the next few minutes going over the details of what we just experienced in Elsha's home. Becca said she was scared at first, but she had to guide us to where Nai'Jae was. I asked Becca if she saw or felt or saw anything else, she said she couldn't remember.

Part of her vision was blocked by darkness, but she was able to use her power to guide them through. Eric wondered if someone was helping us because of the dark ghost we saw. Elsha tried to wrap her head around things but she had to get to her uncle's house before he called her again. She said she would keep trying to reach out to her dad and let me know.

Rocky Point was about a few hours a way I was thinking about taking a drive there. I convinced Elsha to allow me to take her to her uncle's house and she agreed. Once we arrived Police Chief Morgan met us in the driveway. Elsha was first to exit the car.

"Uncle what is going on? I've been trying to reach my dad and he is not answering."

He put his arm around her and told her not to worry.

"Look I know you are worried, I've got a team down there working on getting in touch with him. We were able to reach him by radio; freak storms have knocked out cell towers, so we communicated by radio."

That was a relief to hear, and then he turned in my direction.

"I suggest you kids get going but before you go Kyle, I'd like to speak with you alone for a moment."

I wondered what wanted to talk to me about, however I had no choice in the matter. I asked Eric to stay with Becca while I spoke with Chief Morgan. But Elsha wanted to take her inside to meet the twins.

"Kyle, I wanted to talk with you away from Elsha for a moment. How is everything going with Becca? Is she doing okay? I haven't had time to check up on her since her parents died. Has she said or remembered anything?"

I told him she is doing okay and that she does not talk much about her parents unless she dreams about them. I also explained that she has not spoken about that night nor remembers anything else.

Police Chief Morgan was very sympathetic, even though he could be intimidating. However, I felt he didn't want to talk about Becca, either so I asked him about Dr. Morgan.

He told me that he didn't want to say anything in front of Elsha. It bothered him to shield the truth, but he said he did make radio contact with his brother, but it was lost again. That was 24 hours ago. There had been none sense. He is getting ready to travel to Rocky Point to find him but needed a favor from me. He stated due to the recent events he was also sending is wife and children away for a while and needed Elsha to stay with her.

Which meant Elsha would be gone as well. He said it would be the only way until he found out about his brother. He knew Elsha would put up a fight but with a little bit more reinforcement it would help. I told him as long as he took me and Eric along with him, I would agree to convince Elsha to leave.

"You drive a hard bargain young man, but this is official Police business, what's your interest in this?"

I didn't want to tell him, but I just said.

"You have your ways and I have mine, there are people there I know of that are with Dr. Morgan please let me and my brother assist you. We won't get in the way."

He looked at me rubbing his chin, Chief Morgan was not one to reckon with, but I stood my ground. I turned toward Eric and waved at him to get out of the car. I introduced him to Eric and Chief Morgan said he could definitely tell we were twins.

"Alright young man we leave at dawn, I will pick you up at your house. I will tell let your parents know I need your help a special project"

I explained to the Police Chief that I would be just fine driving. Eric was wondering what mom and dad would think about this. I would have to just tell them the truth but not all of the truth.

Police Chief Morgan explained to Elsha how he needed her to stay with her Aunt Faith a few days at her parents' house with the twins. Elsha was stubborn at first, she wanted to talk with her dad. I told her it would be good for her to go and I would keep trying to get a hold of Ms. Creed.

Elsha loved her aunt Faith, she is like a mother to her and besides she enjoys spending time her twin cousins. It took a while to convince Elsha, but I wanted to ask Police Chief Morgan about the most recent events.

"Tell me Chief Morgan, how many people are missing?"

He hesitated a little bit, and then explained.

"Well son we haven't' got a total yet, but people are getting panicky. This town used to be a quiet one until all of these events started happening. There is only so much I can tell you at this point, but you watch over that little girl. It appears that some of the missing is mostly females."

Police Chief Morgan was so puzzled he lifted his hat scratching his head, and then Faith comes running out of the house.

"Frank you have an emergency call."

He told me he had to take the call he told Faith to have the call sent to his car. Eric and I followed him.

"Police Chief Morgan here go ahead please."

I recognized the voice on the other end.

"Frank it's John, I'm okay, and I'm alright!"

A sigh of relief filled the air. Police Chief Morgan was very relieved.

"John what's been going on I was just about to travel with a search party to look for you."

I was excited to hear that he was doing well also.

"Frank, it's been crazy down here, is Elsha safe."

Police Chief Morgan told him Elsha was inside the house with her aunt and the twins. He was very pleased. Then he asked for a favor from his brother.

"Frank things have been crazy down here I will give you the details when I arrive home. Listen I need to get a message to Kyle Green and have him call me right away!"

Chief Police Morgan quickly responded.

"Well John he's right here, he brought Elsha over a while ago."

Chief Morgan handed me his phone.

"Hello, Dr. Morgan its Kyle."

I was nervous and anxious at the same time.

"Hello Kyle, good to hear from you listen up. I just wanted to let you know that Nai'Jae is awake she is being transported to my hospital. I can't' explain everything now but I will when we get there. She has been asking for you."

I told him with great joy that I couldn't wait to see her. I handed the phone back to Police Chief Morgan; he said he wanted Elsha to know that he was on his way home and for to stay with her aunt and uncle. Police Chief Morgan as his brother if there had been any children disappearing in Rocky Point, his reply was a good one, but he however there had been a few strange sightings from the local natives.

It would something that could not be explained. Police Chief Morgan told me and Kyle to head home with Becca, Tony called and said he would meet me at my house and stay over. I told Elsha I would see her later and that I'm glad her dad called.

Although Nai'Jae was awake, she was still not out of danger. I guess the great spirits decided not to keep her. Well whatever the cause, it was good to have her back. Ms. Creed must be happy as well. On the way home, we Becca spoke about the event, she wanted to know if the little girl she saw was going to be okay. I told her yes, she was I asked Becca how often her visions pull her in like it did at Elsha's and she said. Not often. She explained that he felt weird and heard someone crying out for help.

Eric asked if she saw anything else, she said no it was too dark, but she focused on the little girl she saw. She said she was guided somehow through the darkness until we reached Nai'Jae. I thought about the dark ghost we saw, it kept the shifters away from us just in time to get Nai'Jae's body out.

Who or what it was I do not know; Perhaps I needed to call my uncle Benjamin and speak to him about this. Eric said he has never seen anything like it before either. I didn't want to talk more about it around Becca.

I wanted to have pleasant dreams tonight she has been through so much and it's hard to escape the things in life you are destined to do. We arrived home in time for dinner. And as usual Becca helped mom in the kitchen and dad talked me and Eric about the news.

He said he was reinforcing the locks on the windows and doors and was going to set up security cameras. He asked me where my gun was, and I told him it was in the lock box. After we helped dad with the house, we had dinner and he said he would finish up tomorrow. I was very tired but stayed up watching movies with Eric and Tony.

Chapter Ten

NIGHT VISITOR

After watching television, I decided to turn in for the night. I was glad that things turned out well for everyone in spite of all of the chaos going on. I'm not sure when I drifted off to sleep my dream started off to be a pleasant one though. I turned over in the middle of the night feeling a little disturbed.

My eyes scanned the room and then I saw it. Something tall, dark and mysterious stood in the corner of my room. Standing as tall as the window, I didn't move and neither did I. I kept my eye on this ghostly shadow. I had no idea why it was there, it helped us when we entered Nai'Jae's nightmare. But why is it here now?

With my head, barely above the blanket, I showed no fear, I just stared at it. Was this another guardian come to watch over me? I wondered along with other thoughts in my mind how long it would stand there staring at me.

When I was a child, I was frightened by what I saw. Watching the night come alive was very scary. Running away from what was in the dark, wondering if I would ever escape.

Being alive is great but the fear of not knowing if you are going to survive the unknown is scary. Because where the sun is rising in one place it's setting in another.

This shadow in my room, had no eyes, nothing about it appeared as a shifter. What is this entity? Why is it here? What does it want? Do I dare say something or ask of its presence? Hours must have past.

I thought perhaps my mind was playing tricks on me. But I knew better, I tried to focus my mind on it. See if I could get through to it. Never taking my eyes off it, I relaxed my mind. Allowing myself to become one with the night, I could feel my body starting to shift. Then it moved and was gone.

I don't know what happened, why did it leave? Who or what was it? Shifting back into my body I ran to Eric's room.

Could I have dreamed this? I was so confused, I've had dreams within dreams before, awake but not awake. I just had to be sure this was real. He must have been out of it, not wanting to wake anyone I entered his room.

To discover a ghostly image hovering over his body surely this was no dream, I pinched myself to make sure I was awake, and I was. I stood there frozen for a moment. Noticing Eric's pouch on the dresser slowly picked it up, reaching inside I grabbed a hand full of the crystallized powder tossing it at the dark ghost.

Nothing happened. I softly whispered Eric's name to wake him. The entity didn't move, closing the door behind me I called out again as I moved toward him.

"Eric, Eric, wake up. He rubbed the sleep from his eyes.

"What I'm trying to sleep, what's wrong?

I wanted to be sure he could see what I was seeing. Slowly walking towards me still rubbing the sleep out of his eyes. Eric was not happy.

"Really Kyle, what is the emergency waking me up at this hour."

I told him to be quiet and turned him in the direction of the dark shadow.

"See it! Do you see it?"

Eric turned his head, and gasped.

"Turn on the light! Turn on the light!"

The light switch was by the door, the dark shadow didn't move. Eric whispered.

"What does it want?"

I gently replied.

"I don't know it was in my room earlier."

Eric and I just stood there in the dark, watching it. I just had to know what it wanted. So I asked.

"Who are you and why have you come here?"

It didn't move nor made a sound. Why it came to us I don't know but I couldn't trust whatever this thing was; Eric and I had to find out.

"You didn't answer my question. Who are you?"

Then in a slow deep voice it spoke.

"No one"

Eric responded.

"Everyone has a name, and just as everything has a beginning. Whatever or whomever you have come for you are not going to get it!"

Eric and I moved closer to each other, I could feel a strong surge of power. While in the darkness I saw it move, ripples moving like black silk. The dark shadow spoke again

"I already have it."

Then it was gone. We stood there silent for a moment. I turned on the light and looked at the clock, it was almost dawn. I scratched my head thinking what it meant by I already had it? Then like a bolt of lightning I rushed to Becca's room Eric quickly followed.

We opened the door and we were relieved to see her sleeping in her bed. Eric wanted to be sure was still breathing until we heard her moan and turn over. That was a relief for both of us trying to figure out what just happened. We were approached by two parents with not so proud looks on their faces. Dad was quite disturbed

"What are you boys doing up at this hour?"

I explained to him I thought I heard a noise, Kyle told dad how I woke him up. We also explained to them we just wanted to check in on Becca. Mom crossed her arms and said she would make coffee since the sun was coming up.

Dad asked Eric and I to either join him and mom for a hot beverage or go back to bed. We both chose to go back to sleep for a few hours and join them later. I didn't mean to wake my parents or Eric, but

I have to find out what this dark figure wanted and what it meant by it has what it came for.

I should have stayed up, but instead I went back to my room. There are many strange forces that penetrate this world. When the dead enters the world of the living it can be very scary. I could hear mom and dad talking down stairs. I decided to get up and go peek in on Eric; I want to know if he has ever encountered such a being.

I walked into his room and his snoring was evidence enough that he was asleep he might get mad If I wake him. I don't know how he could sleep after what we just faced. I guess he has a way of dealing with things. I decided to join mom and dad downstairs when I heard them talking. Dad was in his office on the computer mom walked in with his cup of copy.

"Here you go dear be careful it's hot."

Mom sat down next to dad she asked what he was up to.

"What are you searching for honey?"

Dad kept scrolling through the last few hours of and explained.

"The boys said they thought they heard a noise. I figured I'd better check the cameras around the house."

Mom watched as dad scrolled through the videos then he paused.

"What the hell is that?"

Mom also looked as dad pointed out something to her.

"Look there, standing in between the two trees in the backyard."

Mom leaned in for a closer look.

"What dear I don't see anything?"

Dad enlarged the screen, and mom shrieked nearly spilling her coffee

"Aaaggh! Oh my God. Tom, who is that?"

Dad slowly responded.

"Not who Helen but what, it does not have a face."

Dad tried enlarging the image more he wanted to see if the trees were hiding the identity of this unknown person.

"It's hard to tell, but I'm going to send this over to Police Chief Morgan right away"

Mom and dad kept looking over the timelines and noticed that the image. Each caption shows the figure standing between the trees but never moving.

I wondered how such a thing could be on the outside and the inside of the house at the same time.

Instantly dad sent the images over to the Chief of Police. I didn't want them to know I was listening, so I hurried and went back up stairs.

Becca was just waking up telling me she had a strange dream. Eric was also just waking up. I told Elsha to freshen up and meet me down stairs for breakfast and we would talk later. Becca didn't want to wait.

"No brother we must talk now."

Eric asked what was wrong. Becca looked around to see if mom and were around. I told her not to worry they were down stairs. Becca told us about her strange dream. She said she felt a presence in her room last night. She knew something was there, and she wasn't sure if it was real or a dream.

Becca continued.

Chapter Eleven

DARK SILHOUETTES

"Last night I was dreaming peacefully. Then someone entered my dream. I felt it watching me. Everywhere I turned I could see a dark figure of a man. I tried to wake up but it was hard at first. When I tried to open my eyes, I caught something in the corner of my room. The same man in my dreams was now in my room. I prayed for help then it was gone."

Eric and I looked at each other then he spoke to her.

"Little sister, what did it look like, can you describe him?"

Becca nodded.

"Yes, it was tall, dark looking and it had no face."

We encouraged her not to worry and we would keep her safe. I sent her downstairs to get breakfast and told her we would join soon. This was serious and I couldn't make out what was happening. It didn't appear harmless, but why is it watching us? So many questions plagued my mind. I told Eric about what I overheard mom and dad talking about. I didn't know what my dad was going to do next but I explained to him whatever he hears to just act surprised.

As we went downstairs, Becca was at the table eating breakfast. Mom was pouring herself another cup of coffee.

"Good morning boys did you sleep okay?"

We both replied to her.

"Yes mom, yes Mrs. Green very well."

I asked where dad was, and mom stated in his office looking at video recordings from last night. She said it was the creepiest thing she had ever seen. She thought perhaps her eyes were playing tricks on her. Thinking that she was seeing images that were there but technically not or thinking she saw something, but she was. Well welcome to my world mom your guess is right.

We sat and had breakfast with mom and Becca then dad came in from his office with a serious look on his face.

"Tom are you alright? What's wrong?"

Dad looked at all of us and didn't say a word. Mom placed her hand on his arm.

Tom you're worrying the children and me what's wrong?"

Dad smiled and shook his head.

"I apologize about my behavior; I didn't mean to alarm any of you. I have been thinking and I want to send you all on a little vacation before the new school year"

This caused a stir, but I knew dad meant well. He said it's the only way to keep us safe. He said he didn't want to separate me from my brother, so he said Eric could also come along. We debated on this for a while and the doorbell rang Dad said he would get the door.

We talked amongst ourselves for a moment. Mom didn't want to scare Becca, so she tried to talk around her at the table without disclosing too much. Becca already knew so she told mom about her dream. She said she saw a man watching her while she was asleep. Mom didn't say a word. Dad walked in with Police Chief Morgan and they went into his office. Mom told us to finish our breakfast while she excused herself from the table. Giving Becca a very questionable look I wanted to know why she told mom.

"Why did you tell her that?"

Becca glared back at me.

Because I felt comfortable in telling her about it, and besides I felt she needed to know even if she isn't convinced that what she saw was real. While mom and dad were in the other room, I told Becca and

Eric what dad saw on the video. Whatever this was it somehow it was inside and outside of the house at the same time. Unless there were two of them, they even wondered how it could be possible.

I guess I can't be too upset with Becca, mom was always understanding even when I had bad dreams. She always found a way to comfort me and she's always there to help. I didn't want to go away and neither did Eric, we had a lot to do.

I remember I needed to speak with Dr. Morgan. I wondered how Nai'Jae was doing.

Reaching for my cell phone I received a call from a familiar friend. I quickly answered.

"Hello"

"Kyle, Veronica Banks listen I don't have much time. Can you meet me at my place?"

I was very much surprised to hear from her.

"Sure, what's up?"

"Kyle, I got some news and I need to talk to you can you get away?"

She sounded very serious on the phone, so I agreed to see her. Eric questioned me.

"Hey who was that and where are you going?"

I told him I would explain, and for him to stay while I left.

"Oh no, you're not leaving me here to explain nothing for you I'm going."

I didn't have time to argue, I told Becca to tell mom and dad I would be back later.

"Okay big brother."

I quickly grabbed my wallet and headed out the door. I'm glad Police Chief Morgan parked on the street. I know dad was showing him the video. I can't be sent away just yet. I told Eric how I came to know her. I told him it happened one night I left the library on my, the sounds of howling wolves and the chase.

After I was rescued, I was given a knock out drug, so I wouldn't know the location of where I was being taken. I didn't go into a lot of detail, but Veronica broke the story on illegal adoptions of children from the reservation. My mind was plagued with the events of that night; even driving down that stretch of road was even scarier during the daytime. I remembered the landmark to where I was supposed turn.

Eric was trying to call Uncle Benjamin; he's been out of town for a while. He usually checks in on us I hope he was doing well. Turning off the main road Eric was fascinated about the house, He said he had an odd feeling but couldn't quite tell what it was. I know that feeling, the feeling of being watched. I remember Uncle Benjamin staring out of the window long and hard that day. Since my transformation on the reservation one can only wonder what other secrets I don't know about.

Eric said he would like to know why we are being visited by the thing with no face. He asked if we should be worried. We both know it wants something but whatever it is we must find out. Once we reached the house Lou met us at the door, he said Veronica was waiting in her study for me. Lou did a double take when he saw Eric.

"Wow two of you, how about that."

We followed him through the study to where Veronica was. She was on the phone with someone waving at us to come in. As she finished her call we sat down and noticed her desk filled with reports about vanishing people and missing children. Her headlines read about a witness who was in the room when one of the children went missing.

She was only 8 years old about Becca's age. She described a talk dark figure in the corner watching them. The dark figure hovered over her and then she disappeared. Why did it take her I wondered?

Veronica finished her phone call and thanked me for coming. She said she needed my help. But not before introducing herself to my brother she said she didn't have much time to talk. Recent events of missing children have caused panic amongst some of the tribes. She has been investigating a story about disappearances in the last two weeks. She said no one seems to know what's happening or they are just too scared to talk.

She asked me if I had heard or seen anything out of the ordinary. Really, she would ask me that. I know she could be trusted and wondered why she was so interested. But I decided to tell her what Eric and I witnessed. But I wanted her to tell me more first.

Veronica stated that the disappearances were happening during the late hours. Some adults were missing also. She said she has been trying to reach out to the Chief of Police, but he won't comment. Strange events plagued this town like an omen. Community church leaders offer prayers and vigils for the victims and their families. Other stood on street corners holding up signs that the end is coming.

Some believed in the stories while others doubted. Local psychics were cashing in on the weak and scared.

"Anything you know would be helpful."

I explained what we knew

"All we know is that it seeks out individuals, why we don't know or for what purpose."

Veronica leaned back in her chair and took a folder out of her desk and handed it to me.

"What is this?"

Looking over the information inside it listed both Eric and I when we were patience of Dr. Hill. There were reports also on other children who claimed to see a dark figured no faced being during their sessions. I gave her a long stare.

"How did you get this information?"

Shaking her head, she said.

"It wasn't easy; the Good doctor still owes me few favors."

Eric and I continued going over the information. Several reports from other children also indicate other sightings. Some go as far back as thirty years or more. According to the Dr. Hills notes, he thought Eric and I both were seeing the same thing, but he was not quite sure.

I asked Eric about his visit with Dr. Hill and what he remembered. He just said before the doctor could see him Chief Spearhorn showed up and took not only him but other Native American children. He didn't know about me then, but it all made sense. Eric says he remembered Chief Spearhorn and a few others had a list of names.

Later he would find out that several other children talked about seeing dark images, but none revealed the one without a face except for just a few. He also said there was talk around the reservation of stories about this figure being seen. The elders don't talk about it much, but it makes him wonder.

Veronica told us that she was planning a road trip to a small town just about thirty minutes away. She said we were welcome to join us, and she would have us back way before dinner. Eric and I agreed. She warned us that it's a small ghost town near Harshaw where we will stop first. A source told her where she could inquire more information.

Lou came in and told Veronica the car was gassed, stocked and ready to go. I asked her who she was meeting with and she said she wasn't sure, yet she was to wait for a phone call. I didn't like the way it sounded but no need in her going alone.

I left my car at her house and we drove out of town. I explained to her that she should be more careful, but she says Lou always travels with her. As we headed out of town, Elsha called to see what I was up to she says her dad has not left the hospital since he's been home. I told her I was a little busy and would call her later. I didn't want to go into detail about what I was up to but I think she already knew.

Apparently she was in town and ran into my mom and Becca, she said for me to call her dad as soon as I could. Nai'Jae was improving but still asked about me. I started to feel bad, I asked Elsha to see if she could take calls. I would love to speak to her, so she could hear my voice. Elsha suggested I call her dad, he could make the arrangements. I told her I would call him right away.

Veronica asked if everything was alright, I told her yes. I didn't want to go into any further detail or have Veronica trying to get access to Nai'Jae, so before calling Dr. Morgan I told Veronica that what she was about to hear was private and not to be published. Unless I choose to reveal what more I knew. She just wanted the facts and to learn more about the strange events in our town.

She said she sensed a little distrust in my voice and that I should trust her by now. Even though she was right perhaps I am protective a little and Veronica wanted to know something she had ways of finding out.

We talked for a while and Eric mentioned that he is considering leaving the reservation. I asked him why and he said he feels compelled to and to stay with me if it was okay with my parents.

Chapter Twelve

DISTURBANCE

He said dad seem to have extended an offer when he mentioned sending me and Becca away before the next school term. Eric said he is comfortable being at home with me and Becca is such a sweet little girl. I decided to go ahead and call Dr. Morgan he answered quickly.

"Hello Kyle, glad you called I've got an update on Nai'Jae's condition. There was a brief turn of events last night and this little girl said she had a strange dream that she does not want to discuss with me but only with you."

I asked Dr. Morgan if I could speak to her and he said she was headed home with her mother he had planned on visiting them within the hour and asked if I could meet him there. I didn't' want to bail out on Veronica like this so I explained as soon as I saw Nai'Jae I would meet up with her later. She said she had a few more calls to make and gave me the directions. She said reassured me that Lou would accompany her there and there was no need to worry she was not going alone.

I confirmed the time with Dr. Morgan and headed over to Ms. Creeds house. When we arrived it was already noon, I called my parents and explained, and dad didn't want us out to late. He reminded us of curfew and he said the Police department was cracking down on people being out late past curfew.

We went up to the door and we were met by her parents they escorted us in and we waited the study. Ms. Creed's house always had a warm feeling about it. I remembered the last time I was here looking at her art collection and figurine statues.

Although she had quite the collection, they were something to look at. Ms. Creed entered the room and greeted us. She looked somewhat relieved to see us although she still looked concerned. She told me that Nai'Jae was resting in her room and was waiting to see me Ms. Creed and Eric sat in the living room.

I gently knocked on the door and there she was lying in her bed. She sat up in the bed and said she was very glad to see me. I asked her how she was feeling, and she said much better until last night. I asked her to tell me what happened she trembled a little and explained.

"I was so scared; I never want to dream like that again. It was horrible.

I adjusted her pillow for her and told her to continue.

"I don't know where to begin. I was in a strange place I could hear many voices, but I couldn't understand them. I didn't know where. I was not alone I felt something, or someone was following me I could feel it."

I felt bad having her relive this, but this is what she wanted. I assured her she was safe now and told her she didn't have to go on if she didn't want to. But she had a very courageous spirit.

"I walked in this unknown place until I saw a little light. As I walked toward it, I felt a dark shadow creep over my shoulders, and then I saw him. A tall being without a face."

Struggling to talk I picked up her glass from her night stand and gave her some water. I asked her what she saw. She said the man with no face or whatever it was.

She said there were children held in suspension and he pulled essence of light from the air placing it in their mouths. The children seemed to gasp for air then each child disappeared after that. Nai'Jae continued.

"I couldn't move. I was paralyzed. Then I saw someone else, someone even scarier."

I encouraged her to continue.

"Who, who did you see?"

She took a deep breath and said.

"A horrifying man with burnt skin, he was very mean. He watched the one with no face and couldn't cross the barrier. The one with no face was not hurting the children but hiding them. And then he saw me and spoke in a native language, transforming with the night. I couldn't move, his long claws came at me and then someone else appeared."

I couldn't believe this little girl dreamed of the Suhnoyee Wah, and ancient killer of our people. It seemed as if there is no escaping him. Only the bravest can survive him. Nai'Jae had an overwhelming power illuminating around her. She appeared to mature more right before my eyes. She continued with her dream.

"The dark-skinned man with the blue eyes blew circle of smoke around me hiding me from him. He didn't speak but he showed me many things. I saw you as a warrior from long ago fighting against the Suhnoyee Wah. You moved like they moved and transformed as they did. He even showed me how powerful you are. The man with no face is a seeker of the gifted ones; his identity is unknown."

Nai'Jae described be wearing warrior clothing, she even talked about seeing the two twin boys born but separated at birth. She also described seeing ancient symbols on the dark-skinned man glowing and some merging together. With his staff he drew a circle with triangular points on the inside.

Each point represented a location and each one glowed brightly. The constellation of the stars was in the center. She didn't know what it meant but she said she was hoping I would know. She also mentioned a huge stone with many symbols around it; she described it as a tomb.

I quivered in my seat as she spoke. Nai'Jae talked more about the dark-skinned man. I reflected on my dreams of him and how he saved me. She said the symbol above the stone was the same as on my brow in the dream. It's very powerful and only the one with the eyes to see the pattern in the stars can make it. I asked if she remembered anything else and she said no. She told me how safe she felt with me and she could feel something was coming.

I asked her if she had dreams before and she said yes. She mentioned how her grandparents watched over her at night and prayed. Sometimes she could hear whispers in the wind like voices calling to her. I knew how she felt. Her mother knocked on the door and entered the room. She asked her daughter if she was feeling better and she said she was much better. Ms. Creed told her to go the kitchen and she would join her for lunch.

Ms. Creed didn't even have to ask me, but I did share little details. I told her pretty much what she already knew. Nai'Jae is one of the gifted and chosen ones. She too has seen the dark-skinned man as well. I told her not to fear but also use caution. The doorbell rang, and it was Elsha along with her dad Dr. Morgan. He stopped by to visit to visit and to check in Nai'Jae. He was happy to see her in good spirits.

Ms. Creed asked us to join her in her office she didn't want to disturb her daughter while she had lunch with her grandparents. While in her office I explained Nai'Jae's nightmare and shared that they were like mine. What she sees is just a portion of what's coming. I couldn't help but see the image in my head of the huge stone wall I saw in the cave. My gut told me there is something there else in that cave.

Something about the symbols I saw and what Elsha also researched were more than just that. The stone was placed there to keep something in. This deeply disturbed me. Dr. Morgan asked what I meant about what's coming. I told him far worse than what the town has already faced. It is hard explaining the supernatural to people I didn't mind sharing since Dr. Morgan was very open minded about it.

He told me there had been many strange events in Rocky Point that has raised a lot of questions. Some of the people reported seeing many strange things while others dared not talk. He also said there were talks of a great gathering soon to take place. He asked if I knew about it and I didn't want to answer yet. But I told him I would ask Chief Spearhorn. He also told me about something he found and wanted to speak to me in private.

Ms. Creed left the room and Dr. Morgan asked if I would be willing to give a sample of my blood. This was very strange, why did he want it? What was he looking for? I wondered.

"Dr. Morgan why do you need a sample of my blood, what are you looking for?"

Dr. Morgan stated that he noticed some of the victims although not blood related carried almost the same blood type which was very rare as if they were related. He also said he noticed the same trait in Nai'Jae's blood as well. He says he thinks there is a connection somewhere and would like to see if I would volunteer.

I wasn't sure about that, but I told him to let me think about it. It was time to go and I wanted to get home before dark. Eric reminded me that we were to meet up with Veronica soon. Elsha walked in asking if we were doing alright. I told her things were fine and she said Nai'Jae seemed to be doing well although Ms. Creed was still concerned.

Elsha asked what I was up to later and I told her I had a few things to do. She asked if she could tag along for a while her dad was going to be at the hospital and she didn't want to go. I told her it was okay just for her not to say where we were going if anyone asked.

Elsha wondered what I was up to I knew it by the look on her face. I really wanted to leave so we said goodbye to everyone and headed out of town. Elsha wanted to know where we were going, and I told her to meet up with an old friend. Of course, she threw that attitude with me and she said she wanted to stop by her house first, so she could pick up something since we were headed in that direction, I told her to hurry once we got there.

Eric asked me about Ms. Creed's daughter and I explained him how brave she was to even tell me.

"What did she say?"

He wondered also, and said he knew it was difficult for her, but no one will ever understand the things we come face to face with.

I told him that she saw the dark shadow with no face and he was protecting children from the Suhnoyee Wah. So that's what it meant, it had what it came for, I was still puzzled by it. We approached Elsha's house and she said she would hurry. While we waited Eric and I talked for a moment.

"She is very pretty, how come you to haven't hooked up yet?"

I just laughed.

"No seriously I see the way you look at her, what are you waiting for?"

I shrugged my shoulders.

"I don't know man, she is a tough one and she doesn't want to date right now. I respect that about her and besides I enjoy just being friends with her."

Elsha was on her way out of the house when Tony called. He wanted to hang out I really hoped Veronica didn't' mind Elsha and Tony tagging along so we headed to pick him up. Tony was my best friend and I didn't want to neglect our friendship, but things just kept getting weirder in our town. Patagonia was such a nice place until my nightmares became a reality. I wondered if there had been any other strange disappearance before all this started.

We picked up Tony headed east about a half an hour out of town. We stopped at little, country store filled the car up with gas, grabbed some drinks and snacks. There was not going to be another service station so better to do it now. The scenery was very beautiful, old abandoned homes and building sure gave signs of a ghost town.

We started on our journey again and Elsha wanted to know what we were doing way out in the boondocks. I told her I was meeting up with Veronica Banks she had a lead on a story and I offered to accompany her. This didn't set well with Elsha Erica looked at her and laughed.

"What are you laughing at?"

Eric sarcastically replied.

Sounds like a little bit of jealousy to me."

Oh boy here we go. Elsha waived her fist at Eric then Tony joined in. The next few minutes were just them going at each other until I saw Veronica's car up ahead. We met up with her and she said she was waiting for instructions from a source. Big Lou was sitting in the car. Tony asked what was going on and I briefly explained that we are just here to assist her. I explained she was working on a story.

Elsha leaned forward.

"What story?"

I told her a few events had been taking place and we just need to get some answers. I asked Elsha if she had heard of anything new and she said, she overheard her uncle talking about a few sightings she grabbed her book and pointed out a few things that was all too familiar.

"This is what I wanted to share with you. People have all kind of sightings they report. Different tribes and cultures reported seeing some of the same things but interpreted them differently."

I felt a deep disturbance again. Something shifted inside, Eric felt it as well. Veronica motioned for us to follow her. We drove we took a path onto a dirt road, driving by historical monuments. Clay shacks covered by tall weeds damaged by time and war, even the mines looked creepy. We came to a small pioneer town and parked in front of an antique store.

Chapter Thirteen

Signs

A small group of people gathered out front waved to us we smiled just to show a friendly gesture. An elderly gentleman approached us. He wore a black hat and had long silver hair. He had the cowboy look and huge belt buckle to match.

"Hi and welcome to Harshaw County, my name is Henry Jones we don't get much folks up this way except for a few locals and tourist. Which one are you?"

Veronica told him we were locals but just looking for someone, she gave handed him her business card and he said.

"Oh, you must be the reporter lady. My son asked me to wait here until someone arrived. He's down the way there in the building at the end. He runs a small business and is expecting you follow me, and I will lead the way."

He seemed to be a nice gentleman. As we walked, he gave us a brief history of how rich the town used to be. He said people would come from miles around to dig for gold, buy and sell goods. He even told us how rich the soil was planting gardens. Eric asked what happened and he said wars, famine, droughts came stripping the land of everything. People couldn't afford to live here anymore so some headed further east, while others west. The lakes dried up and some feared a great curse was placed upon the land.

Elsha was so touched she questioned.

"What made the people think there was a curse upon the land?"

Henry raised his hat scratching his head.

"Well young lady many believed it was due a myth about an ancient warrior getting revenge on the descendants that killed him."

I couldn't believe it, Eric and I just looked at each other. Henry talked about ancient curses, superstition, rituals to help heal the land. This really sparked my interest along with everyone else's. We arrived at the building, and Henry pressed a button on the door. A woman's voice answered on the other end and Henry told her that there were visitors. A buzzing sound came from the door and the door unlocked.

"Well folks go on in he's waiting for you. If any of you wanted a tour just let me know I would be glad to show you around."

Elsha said she would love a tour, Tony said it would be nice to learn some history. They went with Henry to be shown the town while we went inside to meet this source with Veronica. The building was old and creepy looking. Photos of the town in its prime lined the walls, it even showed pioneer settlers, and army confederates in some of the photos with the local natives.

There was even a school here once; by the way this building was made this must have been it. We took the service elevator up to the floor. We came to a reception area we were met by a young lady with blonde hair. She spoke with a bit of a southern slang.

"Hi, Mr. Jones has been waiting for you, just have a seat and he will be out in a minute, can I yall something to drink while you wait?"

We all declined and thanked the nice receptionists while we waited.

Then a door opened, and a tall brown-haired gentleman approached.

"Hi, my name is Bill Jones, nice to meet you."

Veronica introduced herself and us. We shook hands with the gentleman and he ushered us into his office. He asked the receptionist to hold his phone calls and make airline reservations for him while he met with us.

Veronica inquired of his trip.

"Going a vacation?"

He sat down in his chair, putting papers in his briefcase.

"No just more field work. I understand that you are seeking some information, may I ask what kind?"

This guy didn't waste any time, he got right to the point. Veronica explained to him about her research and how she was told he could provide it. He said it all depends on what she was looking for. She explained she had been doing research on children who had been experiencing odd dreams, or sightings of something paranormal.

Bill told her that she should not waste her time following ghost stories. But it seems that he had also done his homework on her as well.

"It seems that you disappeared for a while, did it have something to do with the illegal adoptions on the Spearhorn reservation? Or perhaps you were getting a little too close for comfort. The Spearhorn's don't like people snooping into their affairs you know. And neither do I."

Veronica snarled under her breath, she relaxed herself in the chair and kindly asked the gentleman what he knew, she told him it's nice that he can dig into her past, but she did explain her relationship with the Spearhorn's is not soured but of a pleasant relationship.

"So are you going to tell me what I need to know or what?"

Bill seemed as if he was hiding something, He told her it doesn't make sense to feed her emotions with ghost stories. I didn't like this guy. He went on talking about the town's history, and how it was such a thriving place long ago. He also talked about new land development from outside investors. There may have been some miscommunication here. The way he talked was as if we were there to buy real-estate.

Veronica asked if he knew why they were meeting. Bill said it was to get some history on the town to inquire about some investment opportunities. Apparently, this guy was out to make a fast buck. I didn't like him. I could hear Eric crack his knuckles every time he mentioned the Spearhorn's. It's evident enough we are meeting with the wrong Jones. I have a feeling the real person we are to meet with is giving Elsha and Tony a tour. I quickly interrupted their conversation.

This guy doesn't like reporters nor does he like people asking questions. He wants to be sure that no one jeopardizes what he is trying to accomplish. Veronica explained she is not here to discredit his ability to sell real-estate she was just following up on a lead.

"Perhaps we should just look around first. My parents are looking to buy investment property surely this would be a good time to take some pictures and go from there."

This seemed to please the man. But I just wanted to get out of here. He thinks she is here to uncover a hidden plot but that is not the case. She thanked him for his time and told him how he she didn't want him to miss his flight.

We walked out of his office and headed to the elevator. Surely this was a miscommunication Veronica tried to get a hold of her contact but received a voicemail. I told her not to worry we would get some answers. We headed back to the antique store where we met up with Elsha and Tony.

Elsha was very excited; I could tell she had a lot of news to share. And Henry was about to give them some history on the town. I considered this perfect timing and so did Veronica. When Henry joined us, he asked how everything went and If we had planned to buy. Veronica explained to Henry she was just a reporter looking to get information on Native American history. Henry laughed.

"Well young lady I do apologize, I was told someone coming to find out about the land. If I had known that I would have told you anything you needed to know. What can I help you with?"

Veronica explained she was researching children who reported seeing a strange phenomenon that may have led to some disappearances. Henry stared at her for a minute, and then he looked at me and then Eric.

"Uh, huh, I see. Well follow me young ones."

We followed Henry to an historical hut that was centuries old. Looking around he made sure no one was following us.

"Wait here I will be right back."

I have no idea what this was all about, but it was weird. I looked out of the window and Henry was talking to his son. He was in his car and it looked like they were arguing. Henry took off his hat waiving it at him. Then Bill drove off spinning his tires.

Henry entered the hut apologized, he said sometimes the smell of money clouds his sons mind. He asked us to each sit down on the rugs and he would tell us a story. He said he chose the hut because when he was a young boy this is where he would sit and listen to the Elders tell stories about his people.

He asked that we not record him, but he allowed us to take notes. Elsha already had her notebook ready to go and Veronica pulled out her little black notebook. Eric and I didn't prepare for this, but we were ready.

Henry sat in a rocking chair he said his legs would allow him to sit but down not get up. We all laughed. He started by telling us that during the time when the land was young there had been many stories of strange sighting seen across the plain. He said some people fear that death had come to the land when word of an ancient warrior vowed to kill off our people.

He said there are many stories passed down from generation to generation. Some are more believable than others. Then there are some that hold true to the fact. He said this is what makes our people strong. He mentioned how important it is to hold on to our beliefs preserving the language and our culture. Veronica told Henry that she had been working on a story of a dark figure without a face. She also asked if he had ever heard or if possibly seen it.

Henry rubbed his chin. He said he didn't see it, but he has heard about it. Veronica turned a page in her book to get ready to write down what he was about to say. I decided to talk and share my experience on what Eric and I saw last night.

I told him how it just stood in the corner watching me, I told him I spoke to it, but it didn't move. Then it disappeared only to be discovered in Eric's room. Only then it spoke telling us that it had what it came for.

Henry looked fixing his eyes on me, then Eric.

"*Ekua didanádo* nasgi asgaya uha awadádi nihi." This means.

Great Spirits he has found you."

Henry opened up and gave more details.

"My father once told me of a very strange thing he saw one night. He described it as tall and took the form of a man. He said he was a sleep one night and felt something watching him he didn't know what to do but pray that the spirit guides would keep him safe. No harm came to him but all night he watched it and it never moved. Others claimed to have seen him and thought it was death letting them know their end was near. My father said he doesn't know what purpose it had but it has never brought him harm, but others would argue that."

Veronica asked if there had been any other mysterious things happening and Henry said yes. He could feel there was something happening in the atmosphere that even has the animals stirred.

Looking up at the now greyed sky he said.

"Sometimes the night is too quiet. I just sit and listen for a sound of a mountain lion or coyote. Nothing but dead silence."

Veronica kept questioning him and he kept answering. Then Elsha started.

"How many pioneer explorers traveled through here?"

Henry reached for a book on the shelf.

"Well now let's see here. There were many, some came for peace other came for treasure. But there was one explorer mentioned here oh and he is even pictured with one of my ancestors."

He scrolled through the list of names and found one very familiar.

"Jeremiah Flynn, yep he settled here years ago. Is there something you'd like to know little lady?"

Elsha replied quickly

"Yes, his great, granddaughter is a professor and I am helping her with retracing his steps before his disappearance."

Henry paused for a moment.

"Hmmm, that is very interesting perhaps you should invite her to come I would love to share some information with her."

Then Elsha's persistence kicked into high gear. She wanted to know what he knew so she kept probing. He finally told her that there were many that disappeared from this land. Some thought to be scalped by savage warriors. But there was one that told a different story. She was a great, great ancestor of mine.

That talked about a pale face man that came to visit. He wanted to learn the ways of the Cherokees' and other tribes. His disappearance remains a mystery, but a legend does tell of a pale face written on one of the cave walls here that he perished along with others.

He told us how many people were afraid if they didn't worship the evil their families would not be spared. Some even left the land while others vowed to stay and fight. Eric asked if he had ever encountered a Suhnoyee Wah, Henry said he encountered many things in his life time. Some he never wants to see again. I took that as a yes.

Henry was very knowledgeable and gave us a lot of history of our people. He told us to be strong and be careful. He was about to say something then he paused. Veronica had got what she came for. She asked Henry if she could come back and he told her anytime. The hour grew late, and he told us we should head back before it gets too dark. Veronica and Lou left first. I told her I would catch up with her later.

Elsha asked if she could look at some of the photos in his book. He told her that was fine if she promised to put them on the shelf when she was done. Then he asked if Eric and I could meet him outside. Tony would stay with Elsha and look at some of the historical photos.

Henry had a look of concern on his face; I asked him if everything was alright. He said yes but wanted to know why we are so interested in chasing the past. I flat out told him that past is chasing us. And that we don't have a choice but to keep going. Henry asked our last names and we told him.

He said there was no doubt he could see we were twins but why the difference in our last names. We briefly explained it to him and then he shook as if a cold chill came over him.

I asked if he was alright and he looked out over the horizon pointing.

"Something is coming, I can feel it. There is a shift in the atmosphere that tells me a war is coming. My father and grandfather told us as children that one day we would have to come together to fight a great evil that plagued our land. My children I fear that day is coming soon. I would advise getting your friends and heading home."

Henry was right; war is coming. I peeked in on Elsha and Tony and told them to meet me at the car. I would join them in a moment. Henry had left and headed to down a dirt paved road. Of course, I knew Elsha would not listen, so everyone followed behind me.

We followed Henry past a few buildings to a little hut in the back of the antique store. Peeking through the window we saw two old native women sitting in chairs weaving. There were many beautiful crystals hanging from the ceiling. Henry spoke to them in native language and one of them never looked up. Elsha whispered why we were listening instead of going in. Before things could get any awkward one of them spoke.

"Tell the children to come inside."

The door opened, and Henry met us. He told us to come in and have a seat. We were welcomed by the women as we watched them weave what appeared to be dream catchers. The first introduced herself as Milieah, the second Tilieah. They too were twins. It will be dark soon in these parts, so I didn't want to waste time. Milieah spoke first.

"You have said right young man, it will be dark here soon there isn't much time. Tell me what information do you seek?"

At first, I didn't know what to say until I looked closer at how she weaved the dream catcher. A perfect circle outlined with triangular crystals. When I kneeled down for a closer look, she revealed something that sparked my interest in what I already knew.

"What does this symbol mean?"

With her wrinkled hands Milieah explained each point represents the stars of the spirit guides. Across the bottom and the sides are the boundaries, the first circle represents the universe and the second a parallel world. Each crystal represents a boundary can be read just like a map.

It acts as a seal to protect the living and capture the evil. She continued telling us how this technique was used centuries ago to place on the foreheads of the mightiest warriors.

A circle would be drawn on their foreheads and diamond points to connect with the stars. Only someone who was gifted to look at the map in the stars could see the symbol and create them. Others wore different symbols on their chest.

Then Tilieah told us what she knew.

"For years we have watched the stars and they have shown us the way. Heaven has a huge map; if you read it correctly it will get you to your destination."

I just had to ask them about the symbol I saw in the cave. I was hoping they would tell me what it meant. My curiosity wanted them to reveal more of the truth.

"I once saw a symbol like this deep in a cave; there were other odd shape symbols around it. The circle was big and a triangle in the center. The symbols seemed to be like spells to keep something in. Can these same symbols you weave your dream catchers with be used to seal an evil spirit?"

Both women looked at me and paused.

"Can you draw the symbol from memory?"

That image will also be with me. I took some paper and drew the symbol and showed it to the women. Elsha also showed the women the same seal from photos she took in the cave. Milieah and Tilieah looked at each other and nodded. Milieah explained her knowledge of the symbol.

Chapter Fourteen

THE READING

"This is more than a symbol Kyle; this is a seal of the Suhnoyee Wah. It was forged from silver stone centuries ago placed there by the chosen ones. Each selected from a sacred tribe placing a seal of the seven sacred prayers over the tomb."

Milieah asked me to extend my hands with my palms up. She asked Eric to do the same. Both women walked around us closely examining us, I wondered what they were looking for. Milieah looked at Tilieah and spoke what her twin was thinking.

"There is way to tell dear sister, only one way to be sure. Please young men come with us."

Eric asked where the women were taking us. Tilieah explained as we followed them.

"It's time for you to learn more of who you are."

She opened a room in the back where another woman sitting in a bed she also was weaving, and she was very old. Her wrinkled hands shook as she weaved an even perfect circle with a small needle. She had long silver hair and her eyes were blue as if she was blind. With a soft gentle voice, she spoke.

"Thank you, dear ones come in young men and close the door. I have been waiting for you; destiny has brought you both to me."

I stepped forward.

"Who are you?"

The old woman stopped with her needle.

"Ah, you are Kyle the first born. Come forward. When the time is right, I will reveal my name."

I asked myself how she knew who I was. There seems to be something about this woman that puzzles me. I slowly moved toward her.

"Come closer son, don't worry I won't bite."

Eric and I just looked at each other as I moved closer to her. She asked me to hold out my hands, so she could take a look at me. But I don't think she could see me. She appeared to be blind. She asked if she could feel my face.

I leaned forward while she caressed my face. Then she caressed my hands and gently ran her fingers across the lines in my palm.

"You are the strong one, born first. Even when your mother was attacked you were hidden by the guardians. Both you and your bother Eric were protected; the Suhnoyee Wah could not get you. Although you mother perished, she died so you could live."

How did she know this? I asked myself. Then she answered.

"Oh, young brave I know many things. I can see with more than my hands you know."

Eric asked the woman who she was, and what she knew about us. The woman sat back on the bed also asking him to come closer.

She read Eric the same way as me and told him he was second born. She explained the lines in our hands are like two river streams connecting to each other in a way that can only be read by someone with a true gift.

She pointed out the diamond shapes in between our palm lines represent the lineage of which we come from. She told us that she was from the same lineage, with her shaky hands she showed us her palms and compared the lines.

"Your story goes back centuries, when one of your great, great, ancestors gave birth to two twin boys."

Now she really had out attention. She told us about the evil warrior plaguing the land, vowing to get his revenge on those he felt betrayed him. Certain rituals were done first to determine the separation.

If it was determined, then the boys were to be taken to distant villages to be raised not knowing about the other until a certain time. There was no other choice it had to be done. For centuries twin boys born were to be kept apart especially those who bore certain birth marks.

I asked if any were ever found or if any were reunited. The woman continued.

"Some of them perished before being born. Others would be reunited later when they became of age. But you two are very special. It was wise for both of you to be separated until you found each other.

You two are much stronger together than apart. If he could get you two separated, he will try to find your weakness and kill you. The Suhnoyee Wah is very cunning; it uses the elements of the earth to shield itself. Hiding deep in the darkness, waiting, when to strike its next victim."

She continued giving us more information about our ancestry. I wish she would tell us who she is, but I guess it didn't matter. Eric and I already knew enough and know what we must do to stay alive. But what the woman said to us next I wasn't so sure we could.

"There is a great cloud coming to cover this land in total darkness, the Suhnoee Wah has gathered his army to fight the forces of the living. War is coming and is inevitable our people must stand together and fight this evil. The stars have shown us the way, so we must go to where the earth meets the sky."

Even though we already knew what was coming. The woman asked me to do something odd. And that odd thing was to take off my shirt. I asked her why, she said when a person is injured by a Suhnoyee Wah it leaves a deep scar sometimes if doesn't heal and sometimes it does. She was very persistent.

I removed my shirt and she asked me to lie down on a table while Eric helped her to her feet. Her hands caressed my back I was very confused. Although it's funny Eric never mentioned any marks on his back.

She asked me if I had any pains recently and I told her none that I had mentioned to anyone. With her hands she caressed my back running her fingers along the scars. Her body jolted as she touched me. I could feel the vibrations in her hands then she read my scars.

She described a beast with massive claws sent to destroy me. She said its sole purpose was to drain my blood. Scrolling her fingers in the middle of my back she paused. I asked her was everything okay and she told me not to move.

As she spoke in a native language, she told a chilling story. She said each line meant the generations in the blood line and those of the lives the beast had taken. She told us how the blood is very strong amongst the generations. War was definitely coming, and we had to prepare ourselves.

She wanted us to come back alone; there is something very important that must be done. She warned us about the rise of the first full moon and how more strange things will happen. We walked back to the front where Tony and Elsha were waiting. I thanked everyone for their time and we headed home.

"What happened in there?"

Tony was very curious, I explained to him and Elsha everything was fine. Elsha said she contacted Professor Flynn and she had planned a returned trip. Knowing that her great grandfather passed through these parts was very exciting to her. Elsha wanted to know if she could help me and Eric with anything.

Eric just told her that she needs to stick with the curfew, we all did. An odd feeling came over me and Eric felt it to. Impulse made me drive a little faster; each winding turn getting out of this place was a maze. Once we got onto the main road, we were well on our way, it would be getting dark soon, so I had to hurry.

We decided to take Elsha home to her dad then Tony, once we arrived home. The house was vacant. Mom and dad left a note that they would be back before dark. Eric and I sat down to talk about the old woman. He went first.

"Who do you think she is?"

I told him I didn't know, he asked me what I felt when she read my scars. I told it felt weird, I asked Eric if he had felt anything and he said he wondered what she saw. We both sat and talked for a while then Uncle Benjamin called. He said he was going to be leaving soon and wanted to stop by. While we waited, I called Ms. Creed to see check on Nai'Jae and she said she was doing better. Dr. Morgan had just left from visiting.

I couldn't help but think about the old woman, Benjamin finally arrived, and we spoke for a while. He said he wanted to talk to us and catch up on few things. I asked him where he had been, and he said he was out scouting.

Eric and I looked at each other. Then I asked him what for.

"What do you mean by scouting? Are you planning on buy some land or something?"

Benjamin just laughed.

"No nephew unfortunately no a friend of mine owns property up in Wyoming and asked if I would come up and check out his land. He feared poachers may have been killing the dear for their antlers in alarming numbers."

I shook my head.

"Well that's nothing new people have been doing that for a long time. I remember doing a report on that for school."

Benjamin laughed again.

"That's the thing with public schools they don't teach you everything."

I looked at him strange.

"What do you mean unc?"

Benjamin explained that sometimes the text books and even the local news does not give the full truth. When there are over whelming reports of animals being destroyed for their antlers or horns it's not always the trophy hunters. He said it's the different type of people that use then for rituals.

Still not convinced I said.

"Perhaps but that still doesn't mean anything."

Benjamin explained.

"When animals are killed for sport, the remains are harvested and certain parts buried for new life can spring up from the ground. But when it is killed for only certain parts and left to rot on the ground it is a waste. But then there are those that carve symbols in the carcass of dead animals claiming the animal spirit this is not good."

Benjamin was right; people do stupid things not knowing what they will get themselves into. They will do anything to keep evil away.

He told us about the gathering taking place in Wyoming, soon. People will travel from miles around to see this event. Tribes from all over the world will meet under the giant mountain where the earth meets the sky.

Hundreds are expected to be there, some have already arrived. Benjamin said fellow natives from the Lakota Sioux, Cheyenne, Eastern Shoshone, Crow, Kiowa and Navajo tribes have been there for weeks praying over the holy grounds. More are expected to join in.

Some fear more attacks could take place, but others seem to think different. I told my uncle about our most recent encounter, I told him I had proof if my dad hasn't removed or erase the video footage.

We went into my dad's office to view it luckily dad saved it. We sat and watched the no face being watching beyond the trees on the outside of the house. Benjamin leaned in for a closer look.

"Great spirits, I have heard of them but never seen one before."

I asked Benjamin how much he knew about them and he said just stories from what he was told as a young boy. He also said someone else knows more.

"I think it's time for you boys to take a little road trip with me. There is someone I would like for you to meet."

Benjamin explained the person he was referring to is a longtime friend of the family. He said he would stop by tomorrow and pick us up. I wanted to share more with him, but I waited. My parents had returned home. Benjamin said he would come back later. Mom needed help with a few groceries and dad said he would later need our help in the garage. Mom asked Benjamin if he would like to stay for dinner and he said he would enjoy it very much.

Becca asked what I had been up to and I told her not much. She told me how much fun she had shopping with mom and dad today. She said they stopped by the police station to see Chief Morgan, she said dad gave him a disc to look at. I had a feeling I knew what it was.

Mom had finished preparing dinner and called everyone to the table. It was nice having Uncle Benjamin over for dinner. Dad inquired about his truck.

"That's a very nice truck you got there."

"Yes she is a beauty, until I have to fill her up."

Chapter Fifteen

Blood Ritual

They both laughed. Table conversation was very good the rest of the night. Dad asked Uncle Benjamin if he had planned to take Eric back to the reservation. Benjamin that is was Eric's decision and it would be good for both us to stay together. Dad was very excited.

"Well there you have it another addition to the family. Welcome Eric."

"Thanks Mr. Green. But I'm not sure how my grandfather would feel about this."

Benjamin enlightened him.

"Well Eric he may give his blessing, or he may not. If he feels that you should remain on the reservation until the next semester then return if you so choose to. As a matter of fact, he was coming by to see both of you today. You can try to persuade his decision but knowing Chief Spearhorn he can be hard to bargain with."

Dad agreed, he said Chief Spearhorn does have a way about him. With that being said, there went the sound of the doorbell. I answered the door and to my surprise it was Chief Spearhorn and Big John.

Mom asked them to join us at the dinner table Chief hesitated for a moment, but mom's gentle smile won him over.

"Please sit down."

Chief smiled, and we made room for him and Big John. Now I haven't seen Big John in a while. I swear every time I see this dude, he gets bigger and bigger. What is he doing sniffing steroids or something?

Dad greeted them both.

"What brings you buy our place."

Chief adjusted his chair and stated he wanted to come by to see how Eric and I were getting along. He said he was leaving town soon to attend a great ceremony and felt it best if we accompanied him.

Mom and dad just looked at each other. Dad responded.

"So where are you going?"

Chief Spearhorn explained.

I will be traveling to Wyoming, every year many of our people come together to attend a great ceremony. Leaders from each tribe must go and I think it would be nice for Kyle to attend.

Eric was very excited although he had never been before. Chief Spearhorn talked about the eagle's dance performed by a few members of the Cheyenne tribe; he said it is a very symbolic dance. Taking an eagle's feather from his hat he explained more about the ceremony.

"The eagle feathers are very sacred although they are used for many reasons. For centuries we have honored the sacred bird. My great ancestors would stand on a high cliff praying while holding an eagle. It was believed after the prayer the eagle would fly away taking the prayers of the people up to heaven. It is an even great honor to wear the eagle's feather during the dance."

Just the talk of the ceremony he even had Becca excited.

"I want to go! Please can I come too?"

Dad told Becca he would think about it, since Becca got sick and they had to cut their trip short on the reservation dad thought it would be a good idea to get out of Patagonia. After dinner, dad asked Chief Spearhorn how things were on the reservation. Chief said things are calmer amongst the people and he had hoped to bring more balance to the communities.

Becca had finished her dinner and mom took her upstairs she wanted to stay and ask more questions about the ceremony. Chief Spearhorn said it was okay he enjoyed answering Becca's questions.

Mom said it was okay but only for little while. Dad asked Chief Spearhorn to accompany him to his office for a moment. I wondered what dad wanted to talk to him about. Or perhaps show him the video. The rest of us gathered in the living room to talk. I just had to ask Big John about his huge muscles; teasing him I punched him in his arm.

Big John just flexed his muscles.

"Nothing but steel his here son."

Eric even joined in on the fun.

"Dude you must work out a lot."

Big John just laughed.

"Nope I eat right, take care of myself and get plenty of exercise."

Nudging me in my chest he said.

"Looks like you have been working out too; sure, you haven't been sniffing steroids?"

Eric and I looked at each other and laughed. Wow how could he have known I said that? Becca also had fun; she enjoyed listening to the stories of our ancestors. But I couldn't help but wonder what dad was up to in his office with Chief Spearhorn. Becca wanted to know more about the ceremonies, but mom said it was time for her to go upstairs. I didn't realize the time; I guess we were having so much fun time just slipped by us.

Finally, Chief Spearhorn and my dad emerged from his office; he shook hands with Benjamin and Big John and said he would be in touch. Dad thanked them for stopping by Chief Spearhorn he would love to see me at the ceremony. Dad said he would get back with him and let him know what he would decide.

Eric and I would walk them out. I knew there was something coming and so did the rest of them. Going to the ceremony sounded like fun, I just wasn't sure if I wanted my parents to go.

Chief Spearhorn told us how very important the ceremony was. He said it would be a great experience for us both. Before he left, he asked Eric how he enjoyed being here with me. Eric told him he liked it very much. He asked Chief Spearhorn if it would be alright if he stayed, he told him that my parents had already extended an offer.

Even though Chief Spearhorn was very strict about our heritage and culture, he made this one exception to allow Eric to change schools. Something in his eyes told us both that it was time for him to let go. Looking up at a star filled sky he pointed upwards.

"The stars shine very bright tonight young ones, but the time will come when no stars will shine."

I didn't like the way he said that. I watched big John help lift him into his truck, then walk over to us.

"You boys take care, and don't worry about your grandfather; he says prayers for both of you because you are part of him. Keep safe I will be in touch soon."

Benjamin said he would come by and pick both us up tomorrow; he too had a look in his eye.

"I'm glad both of you are together, you are family and there is a strong bond that keeps us together. Although we are faced with many challenges its strength that keeps us together."

We said goodnight to our uncle and went inside. Dad was in the living room and mom and Becca were on the floor putting together a puzzle. I wanted to go up to my room for a while, Eric stayed downstairs to help mom and Becca. I checked my cell phone a few missed calls from Elsha and one from Tony.

I called Elsha first. She wasn't doing much just her usual studies. She asked if I had my book handy and I told her yes. We started to compare pictures again. She mentioned the cave and of course a cold chill went through me. I didn't want to talk about that place but there is something there that still puzzles me.

I told Elsha what the old woman said about certain symbols, but something about that stone puzzled me. Elsha said she had discovered more history about Harshaw County. There was a time the land was full of native families, but stories of the Suhnoyee Wah drove them away.

She said the town was full of silver at one time. To ward off evil spirits silver was ground into a fine powder to keep them away. During the night silver powder was placed around the outside of the huts to keep the people safe.

Even Silver ash was placed on the foreheads of little children to keep them from nightmares. She also said after the death of a warrior a stone was placed above his tomb. Depending on the life of the warrior although the stones are very sacred legend says they were made from pure silver. And the silver ash was sprinkled around the grave to the sprit couldn't cross it.

Some say these stories were told to frighten people away because of the silver. But there was more. I felt a strong pull to visit the cave again. I just could not bring myself to ask her to go back there. She nearly died. My gut has never lied to me before; I know what I must do. Even though I knew how dangerous it was.

I asked Elsha if she had ever been back near the cave since we escaped it. She said her dad and uncle would ground her for life. She wondered why I would ask such a thing; I guess my long paused made her suspicious of me.

"What are not telling me Kyle? Don't tell me you are thinking about going back in there."

I hesitated to talk taking a deep breath I explained to her how there was something in the cave I needed to see. She told me I was crazy the cave has been sealed ever since we got out. But then she shocked me with what she said next.

"Except for a small opening, I think someone overlooked it."

I quickly responded.

"What! You didn't!"

Elsha said she only went back once and that was to give thanks for her life. She said she wants to explore new things and make new discoveries. Her research about the cave has even helped Professor Flynn. I didn't want Elsha to know when I planned on returning but I needed to borrow a horse. I had been meaning to ask about Windstar anyway, Elsha wanted to know my intentions.

"What are you looking for in the cave, it's still unstable and not safe."

"Yes, Elsha I know, but something about the symbol above the stone wall drives me to take another look."

I felt an argument coming on.

"Look Kyle since the day we met, your life has been an adventure, if you would have never bumped into me."

I quickly interrupted her.

"Oh, so now you admit I bumped into you. Thanks."

She sarcastically laughed.

"Kyle really I'm serious here you don't need to go back into that cave. Unless you take me with you, I don't have to go inside."

I responded to her immediately, there was no way I was going to do that. I would not want that over my head or a gun barrel in my face from her uncle.

"Elsha I don't want you going near that cave please don't pay any attention to me I'm sure there is another way."

This was going to be a long conversation, although I did enjoy talking with her. It seems as if destiny has brought us together for a reason. I had no idea that she had photos that matched the ones in my book. Over and over again I repeated that in my head. Then it hit me.

"Elsha get you book quick!"

She didn't waist anytime at all.

"Sure, but why"

I didn't have time to go into details, but I asked her to get it quickly. We both spent time on the phone going over photos page by page. She asked what I was looking for and I told her the round stone with symbols above. I kept thinking to myself about what I thought it was. Eric knocked on my door to see what I was up to. I didn't want him to know what I was doing but when he saw my books, he knew I was up to something.

Looking at the photos, the symbol in the cave clearly shows it's more than just a drawing. But I needed to be sure. Something was drawing me to it strong urges pulled me towards it. I just had to know. Elsha mentioned her dad was going to be gone for a few hours on tomorrow it wouldn't hurt to take a quick look inside. I would rather go alone though but how could I without Elsha knowing.

My mind was so bogged with this. Eric felt my distress. I told Elsha I would call her tomorrow Uncle Benjamin was coming to pick up me and Eric tomorrow afternoon. I must go back into the cave it's a risk I must take. Eric looked through my book he was amazed, he told me going back to the cave was a crazy idea. But gut instincts said differently, and he agreed.

Chapter Sixteen

Dangerous Ground

The next day Eric and I woke up early; I grabbed my backpack and headed to the garage. I told mom and dad that we would be back we were going to hang out for a while. Becca wanted to tag along but mom had her on piano lessons to help her cope with the death of her parents. Becca's nightmares had started again and her therapist suggested she do something she loves. Well I guess playing the piano is one of them.

I stuffed camping gear into my backpack. Once I had everything we needed, We headed towards Elsha's house. Eric didn't seem to concerned being that we have faced dangers together before. I just didn't want to get buried alive. Eric asked how I planned to keep this from Elsha; I told him she wouldn't find out. He didn't quite agree.

"How is she not going to know when you park your car in front of her house?"

He was right, but I explained to him the details.

"Well brother, I have been out here so many times I noticed multiple trails that lead to the property it will just require a short hike.

I will have to park about a half mile and we will have to walk the rest of the way. She will never know."

Eric said it was a clever move but knowing Elsha he didn't put anything past her. He said eventually she would find a way. I reminded him not without me, she learned her lesson the first time not to enter anymore caves. I told Eric how I still felt bad because she wanted to help me with my nightmares by finding a solution. I had no idea what she was up to. No one did. I shivered at the thought of the sounds I heard in the cave. I had to get her out to safety.

Eric remembered hearing about it he said as soon as Chief Spearhorn found out he had Big John drive him. Eric said there had been an odd feeling in the air that day. Something didn't feel right.

When I asked him what he meant he said. He could sense danger but he also could smell it in the air. I knew what he meant; we reached a dirt road and turned off near stone lake. The cave was just over the ridge, I parked my card behind a few tree shrubs so it couldn't be seen from the road.

As we walked, we talked more about our childhood and when we first met. It's funny how things happen in life. Impulse must have kicked into high gear as a strong force drew us closer. We saw the no trespassing signs, as we reached the back of the cave. Two huge boulders behind some bushes covered up a hidden entrance.

Eric double checked the gear in our back packs. He checked the supplies we had packed such as rope, battery powered flashlights, flares, water, emergency kits, CB radio. Seems we have everything we need. Then Eric asked if we needed a map and how will we know where to go. I told him before we go in to clear his mind. I told him instinct will guide us right to it. Eric also asked me what I had hoped to find inside the cave. I told him I will know it when I see it.

We made our way through the bushes, just off to the left was a small opening at the bottom. I shined my flash light first to see how far down it went. It appeared to be safe. I tied a rope to the bottom of the bush and dropped it down inside the cave.

We took off our back packs entering the cave on our stomachs. Sliding backwards into the cave I went first. It was deeper than I thought. Once I reach the bottom, I called for Eric to toss his backpack and come down very slow. I shined my light, so I could see him.

Once he reached me. We checked our equipment again. The cave was so dark and cold; we took extra rope and tied it to each other in the event the ground beneath us was weakened. I didn't have time to doubt why I was in here, but I kept going. Carefully walking through the cave going in and out of corridors I came to a familiar spot. This is where I gathered wood to make a fire to keep Elsha warm. Eric took pictures of the drawings on the wall, the deeper we went the closer we got.

I recognized some of the drawings; Eric asked me what I was looking for. I told him to follow the signs on the wall. The ancient ones will point the way. Following the drawings, we made it to the huge stone wall. Right above it was a diamond shaped symbol. Eric shined his light around it and was amazed.

"Brother this looks like a tomb to keep something in."

I felt different about it. I told him perhaps it was to keep something out. As we examined the symbols, I moved my hands alongside of the stone wall. Eric shined his light, so I could get a good look. I told him to be still while I sat on his shoulders, I took a brush and cleaned the dirt away; as I did eerie sounds came from deep within the cave. Eric started to get nervous.

"We should hurry and get out of here."

I agreed, I just needed a few more seconds to clear away more dirt. This was more than I had bargained for. With one last move with the brush, I rubbed my hand over what I thought was a rock.

Slow cracking sounds came from the cave. Sand and rock started to move immediately I jumped off his shoulders and we moved back. We had no idea what was on the other side, we braced ourselves.

It was so dark in the cave, no light but from our flash lights. I fumble through my bag to reach for my lantern.

The light from it was bright enough we no longer needed out flash lights. Pressure from the cave sent a wave of wind at us, we fell to the ground. Once the stone wall completely opened, we stood there motionless. I could feel a cool breeze coming from the inside as we approached with caution.

As nervous as we were something within me told us to keep going. With Eric close by my side we he grabbed my arm before I entered. He reached in his pocket and pulled out a pouch. I asked him what he was doing.

"We are not sure what's in there it could be a burial chamber, before we enter we must put ash on our foreheads just in case. It's a sacred way to show respect to the dead. Never cross into a grave yard whether on top of the earth or beneath it."

Eric pondered what we just entered.

"What is this place?"

Looking around at the skeletal bones on the ground I replied to him.

"You're right brother it's a tomb."

Hanging the lantern on a tree root, we saw all around the room I jumped as something in the corner caught my eye. A skeleton sitting on what appeared to be a throne. I couldn't tell whomever or whatever it was, but they must have been important. The feet were long like claws, hands were attached to long fingers this person was half human half beast. Eric suggested we get out fast.

The skeletons on the ground must have been followers of some kind. We took whatever we could as proof. However, Eric didn't agree with removing anything he suggested not to touch the bones he was ready to leave.

"Brother, whatever this place is we need to get out of here, I'm starting to get a bad feeling about this."

I agreed, I took a few steps to get a closer look, I examine the body which was dressed in warrior clothing, not sure of whom it was. The headdress told a story it was someone of great importance. Right in the middle was a round stone with triangular crossings. This is what brought me here. Eric whispered.

"Kyle, hurry, hurry something is coming hurry!"

Eric stood at the entrance and kept watch, he used my camera to take photos while I grabbed the head piece stuffing it in my back pack. I took the lantern from the wall and the stone moved. Noise from within the cave drew closer. We didn't know if it was wild animals or rodents. Sand and rock fell from above. We didn't have time to search anything else. The stone wall was closing, and we had to hurry.

Exiting the chamber, we headed back toward the entrance. Once we made it, I sent Eric up first. I stood watch until he made it out. Then I climbed the rope after him. Eric told me hurry as he shined the light down. I climbed as fast as I could until I reached the edge.

"Give me your hand, hurry!"

I reached for his hand and he pulled me out. Noise from the inside the cave sounded like a cave in. But noise from the outside of the cave was even more troubling. We looked around and didn't see anything, but we could hear echoes of gunshots.

We could get into trouble if we are caught pass the no trespassing signs, so we hurried back to the car. That was a pretty intense moment alerts from our cell phones told us we were back in service. Eric told me that was the craziest thing he has ever done but it reminded him of when he fell and how alone he was.

Overall, he said he was glad he was not this time. He wanted to see the headpiece it told him to wait until we got back to the car. As we hiked through the woods, more shots rang out, this time a little too close for comfort. Two hunters approached us wearing bright orange jackets, only they wore badges.

"What are you boys doing up here, this place has been sealed off. Eric spoke first.

"We were just hiking sir; we didn't see any signs on the way up here."

They told us to leave, we asked what was going on and he told us wild animals were spotted so hunters are driving them back deeper into the woods. One of them was nearly attacked. He suggested we get moving and fast he didn't want us to get hit by any stray bullets. They were very serious and then curious.

"You boys haven't been near that cave have you; there have been some sightings of big wolves out here."

I told them that we were north of the cave and didn't see anything until we heard the guns shots. I also wanted to know if they were federal agents or something, but I didn't bother. Eric and I left down the hill until we reached the car. I called Elsha to let her know about what was taking place. When she answered I had to be careful and not disclose much. If she knew I was nearby she would question me about the cave.

But after talking with her I didn't have to. She told me how she was having breakfast on the balcony with her dad when they heard gun shots. She said her dad called Chief Morgan to see what was going on. While her dad spoke with her uncle Elsha grabbed her binoculars to see if she could see anything.

She searched the hills but didn't see anything. When her dad hung up from talking with her uncle, she asked what was going on. She said her dad just looked at her and said he was having the horses moved to their other property clear on the other side of town. He would call Rodrigo to come with the trailers and he didn't want her going on any hikes.

Elsha explained that her dad planned on doing some target shooting today, she encouraged me to come over. I told her perhaps later. Eric took the headpiece out of my bag. I told him not to mess with it.

He told me I could get into trouble for taking ancient artifacts he asked if he was going to show Chief Spearhorn I told him not yet. I told him I was going with my gut on this one. Once we made it home, I told him not to say word. He asked if I thought it was safe since we just robbed a tomb which goes against all sacred rules.

I told him I would worry about that later. However; I did wonder if Jeremiah Flynn could be one of the dead? We entered the house through the garage and headed upstairs. We decided to leave our backpacks in our rooms and would go through them later. I couldn't help but think about the cave, what other mysteries it holds. I'm also grateful that we didn't get buried in there, but then again, I felt as if I needed to go back. What is it about this stone? What is the connection?

We decided to grab a snack and watch television before Benjamin arrived. I felt that surge again all through my body. I sunk down into the couch, I didn't feel so well. Eric looked over at me and asked if I was okay.

"Are you feeling okay, you look a little pale."

I tried shaking it off; I told him I would just go to the bathroom and splash cold water on my face. I just stood in the mirror staring at myself, remembering when the last time this happened to me. By back tingled a little and my urge to eat meat increased, I took a few deep breaths to fight the urge. I clutched both sides of the sink very hard.

"Come on Kyle fight it off! Fight if off!"

Breathing heavy I continued splashing water on my face. I heard the doorbell, it must have been Benjamin. I could hear him talking to Eric.

"Hey nephew you guys ready to go?"

Eric said he was ready but was not too sure about me. Benjamin asked where I was and he told him I was in the bathroom. He knocked on the door.

"Kyle you okay in there."

I didn't want to worry him, so I told him I was.

"I'll be right out uncle give me a few minutes."

I had to get myself together, I stood up looking at myself in the mirror, and my eyes seemed darker. Opening the door, Benjamin and Eric stood there. Before they could speak, I told them I was fine. I just needed to grab my bag from my room. Eric said he would get it for me I sat down on the couch putting my head my in hands.

"What's happening to me uncle, I feel my body is going through another change again."

Benjamin sat quiet for a moment he said to let destiny run its course. He said he was not sure what was happening, but he tried to cheer me up.

"I too went through something similar when I was young. Come, we must go now."

I was too weak to stand then a very strange feeling came over me. My back tingled and my head felt weird, the room began to spin, I could hear Eric calling out to me as I fell to the floor.

I felt very hot like my blood was boiling. Eric gasps.

"Oh my god what is happening to him?"

Benjamin rushed to my side.

I could hear them, but I could not see them, I thought I was going blind. My body felt numb. Benjamin acted fast. Tapping my face

"Nephew can you hear me? Kyle, Kyle, come on buddy!"

Benjamin called Eric to his side. As they turned me over small traces of blood stained my shirt.

Acting quickly, they helped me to his truck. Eric wanted to know if what was happening to me would also happen to him. Benjamin explained when our mother was attacked the wound was not deep enough to penetrate her womb. Our mother protected us, but it may have been enough to leave a scar. Benjamin said he needed to get me to Harshaw there is someone there who can help.

"Why Harshaw, we just left there. Why not get him to a doctor first?"

Benjamin drove as fast as he could.

"No time."

What seemed like a short drive felt more like an hour. Benjamin took the short cut, I had no idea there was one. It was a very bumpy unpaved road, Eric touched my forehead and I had a fever. Eric tried to encourage me.

"Hang in there brother, we are approaching the town. Uncle, please hurry!"

Feeling like I was slipping away, I grabbed Eric by his arm, I told him I was holding on. My body was like and inferno, I looked out of the window and the moon soared across the sky. Day turned to night and night turned to day. Sounds from the distance were all too familiar. Voices filled my head as dark shadows moved across the sky.

"Uncle Benjamin Kyle doesn't look so good, how much further?"

Chapter Seventeen

The Cleansing

Benjamin was breaking speed limits like crazy he said it wasn't far we were almost there. Eric turned to me telling me to hold on. Once we arrived, they helped me out of the truck, I felt so weird, but I have had this feeling before but not like this. Henry met us at the door.

"Benjamin, how are you?"

He took one look at me and quickly ushered us inside. Tilieah and Milieah both stood watching they looked at me praying in native language.

Benjamin and Eric took me to a room filled with lighted candles; others were with her softly praying. Everyone in the room dressed in native attire. Henry said he would stand outside the door and not allow anyone in. We exited through a secret passage that took us down a dark hallway where Ancient portraits aligned the brick wall; I hoped I wasn't going to shift again.

But that only happened during an immediate threat. Then again this was a little different, the pain in my back increased so it turned my stomach. I quickly moved toward the wall and vomited blood. As I fell to the floor, Benjamin and Eric grabbed me carrying me into a room that looked more like a place for rituals. They placed me faced down on a table, chaining my arms and legs. Eric was worried he turned to Benjamin.

"Is this necessary? Uncle what's happening? What is she going to do?"

Then a voice came from the back of the room.

"It is very necessary that we do this I'm afraid there is not much time we must act quickly, remove his shirt."

It was the old woman we met yesterday; she had an odd-looking knife and an herb bowl in her hand. She told me not to worry; as she explained what needed to be done.

"This ritual has been done for centuries; the only way to cleanse your blood is to drain out the poison. Your blood mixed when the Suhnoyee Wah attacked you. The more the blood remains, the closer you get to turning."

I was so weak I could barely lift my head. I had to know who she was. Eric placed his hand on my head.

"Be strong my brother I'm right here."

I could feel the sincerity in his voice, and how scared he was for me. Benjamin stood close encouraged me to hold on. Then she told Eric to lay down on the other table she said he would represent the strength of the first born.

Benjamin told him there was no other way. Tilieah and Milieah assisted the old woman; they placed tobacco, sweetgrass, sage, sage grass, yarrow and Juniper in the herb bowl. Then the old woman place leather bindings in my mouth, it was very bitter. She said it would stop the vomiting. They lit the herbs on fire and placed it before me. She told me to inhale slowly; I felt my body began to cool as the medicine spread.

I don't know what was happening, but I felt myself going into a deep sleep. I tried to fight it, I looked over at Eric and they were drawing symbols on his chest, arms and forehead. His eyes big and wide fixed on something. He looked at me and told me to be strong. He didn't move his lips, but I could read his thoughts. I spoke back to him letting him know everything would be fine.

This ritual had to be done, I knew that now, I never told anyone how I have been hiding my pain and the nightmares. From time to time I would dream something new, I even dreaded looking in the mirror. I knew I was slowly changing on the inside. I remembered what Chief Spearhorn once said about letting things control me. My worst fear is becoming something I'm not, but whatever I became when we rescued Nai'Okah must have always been inside me.

The old woman and the others said prayers as white smoke filled the room. Everyone was to clear their minds. The old woman puzzled me, and I wanted to know who she was. The more I fought to stay awake the stronger the medicine put me out. Although I was in and out of consciousness, I was yet awake. Benjamin sat on the floor with his legs crossed with his hands resting on his knees the others joined him while the old woman stood over me.

The old woman took a smudging feather and dipped it in the bowl. She drew symbols across my back and arms. Then she took ash from the bowl and sprinkled it across my back. It sizzled when it touched my skin. Tilieah handed her a beaded sheaf then she pulled the knife out. The knife was made of pure silver with ancient symbols carved into the blade. The handle was brown and bore similar symbols. Holding it up in the air she spoke in native language.

The room seemed to grow dim, and then she took the blade and began the cleansing. With each mark on my back she started at the bottom and moved toward the top. No one should have to endure this. Screams rang out from within the room, ancient ones appeared before me. Milieah blew white smoke in my face visions of the past flashed before me.

Past and present seem to meet up together displayed in the same vision. The room smelled of herbs as more were added to the flame. The tip of the smudging feather was very sharp as she outlined my scars like a tattoo. The remaining herbs were sprinkled over my back and then I felt the pain. My back began to burn with fire I bit down on the leather bands grunting very loud.

The old woman spoke as she took the knife carefully outlining the scars on my back my blood began to drain. Drops of pitch-black blood dripped in a bowl beneath me. Once the smudging was complete aloe and mint leaves were placed on my back. The coolness I felt against my skin was ever so soothing.

They removed the leather from my mouth; I couldn't believe how fast I healed and how much better I felt.

The nausea was gone, and my strength came back to me. The old woman informed me that although the poison in my blood was gone. There was one more thing left to do, a final cleansing of the blood.

As the women and men prepared, we were taken to another room with an open roof, a fire was kindled before us as we each sat down forming a circle. Benjamin removed his shirt flexing his big muscles. Symbols of protection were drawn across his chest. The same was done to me and Eric. This was so evil could not enter, the symbols acted like a barrier to keep evil spirits outs when such rituals were performed.

The old woman explained that her ancestors performed this ceremony on twin boys, once her great ancestors had two sons that were separated right after they were born. Neither of them new of each other until the time was right. If felt this was all too familiar, my mind reflected on a dream of a woman who gave birth to twins.

I did not want to interrupt her, but I had a feeling I already knew the answer to my question. I remained silent until she was finished. The old woman continued telling her story as we waited. She said her great ancestor was a strong woman who dwelt among the Comanche's during the time of peace among tribes.

I silently spoke.

"Lei'liana, I knew it. She must be a relative."

More thoughts came to me as we listened.

"Long ago my great, great, ancestor Chief Iyotaka had a daughter named Le'liana, she was very beautiful and strong. Her father sent her away to live with the Comanche's to protect her from one we call Liwanu also known as Running Bear.

The room was quiet, as she spoke and set the bowl of blood down on an iron piece of metal that sat above the fire. She then took bits of sage and added it to a brown pouch she carried around her neck. Once the contents mixed with the sage, she poured it into another bowl adding more Taking a handful of smudging herbs, she placed this on top of the blood and lit it on fire.

Thick black smoke like silk came up and hovered over it. She just stared at it and no one moved. I have never seen anything like this before. I don't know what she saw, but she waived a staff that had two eagles' feathers on each side, and at the very tip it had a round stone that sat upon it.

Every time she waived the staff over the bowl it grew brighter. Then she turned to Eric and asked him to extend his hand. She took the knife and cut along his palm, she placed a bowl under his hand letting the blood drip onto sage leaves. She did the same thing with Benjamin and then finally herself. Setting the bowls next to each other the smoke began to intertwine.

The old woman stated this is the strength of the bloodline between our tribes. The flame will tell the story and show great strength. It was like watching the battle between good and evil huge flames sprang up from the bowls.

The flames consumed the dark smoke, as it crackled in the air. She explained once the blood has been cleansed and the blood purified then she can read the flame. As we sat and watched her, I had a feeling come over me. It moved from the base of my spine all the way up to the back of my neck. It was so strong it felt like my body was splitting in two. Eric squeezed my hand tightly and whispered.

"Brother, what's wrong? You're trembling."

I just looked at him and shook my head.

"I don't know something weird is happening to me."

Eric told me to keep my focus, his eyes fixed on something and then he gasped.

A dark figure along the wall casted a shadow, one that we had seen before. It didn't have a face, and no one seem to notice it was there. The old woman took a white powdery substance from her pouch and threw it on the fire.

The room was filled with white smoke, and then she read the flame.

"You are the descendants of the great warriors; time has brought you to your destiny. As the flame crackled and sparked. Your blood is strong and was tainted with evil, your bloodline dates back centuries to the early age of our ancestors.

There is trouble ahead that you must face, stay alert young brave, before your birth you were hunted. And even now the Suhnoyee Wah still seeks you. Now that the poisoned blood has been extracted from your body he will seek to have more."

Then the unimaginable happened, I too began to see what she saw as the flame grew bigger and darker, the head of a wolf life spirit appeared looking around at all of us. As the old woman kept reading the flame, she told us that the time was getting closer and we needed to prepare. Many have been with us guiding us to safety long ago a vow was made to watch over the chosen ones with the gift to see the Suhnoyee Wah.

During the time of peace, a group of men were amongst the chosen to watch over them. They were transformed into dark beings that although their appearance was little frightening to some, it was the only way to know the true ones in their search. Now the time has come for us to work together. The blood line is strong there are many of them waiting.

Something about this didn't seem real, but it was. However, something else I saw bothered me. Staring deeply into it, I saw the wars, and death was everywhere. People hunted down and slaughtered like cattle. Then I saw the murders of two people, I tried to shake it off, but it was no good.

The images were very real as the flames showed me Becca's parents were swallowed up by the darkness. A little girl running for her life as the dark mist moved toward her. Then it hit me, that night when the dark being appeared. It told us something. Looking over at the shadow figure on the wall I stood up and spoke to it.

"So that's who you came for? You came for her that night, you came for Becca. Have you been assigned to watch over her or take her away?"

Moving toward me it spoke.

"She has the power within to see, she too has a destiny to fulfill. Her gifts allow her to see more than her mind can imagine. The Suhnoyee Wah is hunting her too, only time will tell how her destiny will end or begin."

I did not like the sound of that, so I questioned it. The old woman told me I should not ask I might not like the answer I receive."

"Who are you? What is your name?"

As it moved closer more was revealed.

"Fused together by time and eternity, we were twins born in a time of peace and war; our father separated us to protect us. For centuries we have walked the earth in darkness watching and waiting. Only when our task has been fulfilled, we can become separated again. We are the descendants of great warriors from the past. Chosen by time our name is nonexistent."

I continued with my question.

"What do you want with Becca?"

Moving away from us and disappearing into a dark corner it spoke one last time.

"It's not that we have come for her, but what we need her to do."

Then it was over, I picked up my bag to leave telling Benjamin and Eric I would wait for them outside. But the old woman asked me to wait. She asked me not to leave; she explained her position and revealed to us what I already knew about her. She said she was named after her great ancestor Lei'Liana which is a name that shows great strength. She explained that all of us should be careful as there will be many more things released upon the earth.

She too was preparing to leave soon to meet up with the others. I asked her how I could protect Becca and she said that I could not it is her destiny and although she is young her gifts are very mature. Just as I dealt with mine, Becca must deal with hers.

I didn't like it not one bit, I remembered how terrified she was when I found her inside the house. No one else has come forward to claim her so mom and dad basically get to keep her. And it is a good thing, she needs me. Lei'Lana also told us that whatever happens I must be strong.

There are many forces working against us but there is also good fighting for us. I needed to get back home. My back was healing fast and I felt much better. Placing my bag over my shoulder, a feather fell from it. Lei'Liana picked it up and asked about it.

"Interesting, where did you get it?

I froze up, I didn't want to tell her where I found it, but she just smiled at me.

"Take care of it dear it holds more power than it looks."

We headed back to the truck but not before she and the others prayed a safe journey for us. Benjamin asked where I got the feathers and I told him, then he asked what was attached to it and I showed him. He said had never see an ancient head piece like it before.

I told him I would rather hold on to it for awhile. How it stayed intact was puzzling to all of us. Benjamin said it was meant for me to find it, so he told me to take good care of it. He said he felt it was going to serve its purpose. Benjamin said he had planned on doing some fishing for the rest of the day but needed to stop at his store for supplies.

Chapter Eighteen

The Pack

He decided to stop since it was on the way. When we arrived at the store we went in to Benjamin's office, he stared up in the sky for a moment. He slightly frowned his face, sniffed the air and went to gather supplies but they didn't appear that they were for fishing. Eric and I both gave him and odd look.

We wondered why he would take crystals, dream catchers and a change of clothes just to go fishing. It didn't make any sense at all. We asked him what kind of fishing he was doing and he just laughed.

"You boys have your way of searching for things and I have my way."

We sat down for a moment, turned on the television to watch as we waited for Benjamin. After he gathered what he needed, breaking news flashed on the screen. We sat quietly and listened.

"This is breaking new from your local television station. A group of forest rangers have discovered several bodies just up past Millcreek road. The bodies were discovered a short while ago and Authorities have cornered off

the area the victims' names will not be released until the families have been notified. Michael Banes reporting more details on the six-o clock news."

We just sat in silence, Benjamin kept packing. I noticed he put a gun in his bag.

"What's the gun for uncle?"

Like I said I have my way of doing things, come on let's go I will take you boys home. My fishing trip has turned into a hunting trip. I was almost certain that he knew something. Eric asked if we could go. But he insisted we remain at home. He would call us later, but I didn't feel led to argue with him so.

On the way to my house Benjamin turned on the CB radio and listened to the conversations. Others were reporting similar stories of strange sightings, he even turned to another channel and we heard a truck driver nearly wrecked his truck due to a huge animal running across the road. He didn't have time to stop nor did he want to get out. The last time a driver got out of his vehicle to access damage after hitting something in the road he disappeared.

I could feel the coldness of fear shadow our town again. Everyone was put on high alert after things seem to have calmed down. Dad was never the same after his friend was killed. Since then he has had mom and me down at the shooting range. And since Eric has been with us dad is planning our next visit, so he can get more target practice too.

The more we listened the creepier the atmosphere became. People were reporting all kinds of strange sightings. Listening to this reminded me of Mr. Peterson and how he described how quiet the night was and how he felt he was being watched. I shuttered at the thought. Deep down I thought to myself was I any different?

I transformed into something that even I can't explain. I moved swift like the wind and fought alongside of huge wolves.

There is a war going on that is going to lead to more deaths. The Suhnoyee Wah's are getting stronger and growing by the thousands. As we listened to more reports across the radio Benjamin gripped the steering so tight his knuckles cracked.

"Easy uncle, I want them just as bad as you do."

Benjamin kept his focus, his eyes fixed on the road I don't even think he blinked at all. I asked him if he was okay, but he never responded. Eric gently rubbed the back of his shoulder telling him to take a deep breath. Benjamin calmed, and relaxed his hands on the steering wheel.

He pulled off to the side of the road and go out of the truck. There was a slight breeze in the air and he began to inhale and then exhale again. Eric and I were not quite sure what he was doing Benjamin turned toward the east mountain his eyes had a cold stare.

"Pay attention, watch and learn. Sometimes you don't have to look for your enemy, the wind will tell you."

A gentle breeze blew in from the north. We watched him inhale and then exhale again. Turning in the direction of the wind Benjamin caught hold of something fixing his eyes on the forest. It's the same look he had when I saw him staring out of the window at Veronica Banks house.

Eric breathed in slightly and picked up a faint scent, for some reason, I couldn't smell anything in the wind at first, but I knew something had either left or is coming and I think it's the latter.

Benjamin panned the forest with his eyes, his muscles were tensing and began to bulge a little, whatever he was fixed on he looked like he was ready to charge at it. But then he relaxed still staring at the forest. A man emerged, he was tall medium build, short brown hair and he wore a ball cap and he a leather necklace with a silver claw attached to it. He was breathing a little heavy and was covered in sweat as if he had been running.

Benjamin greeted him and gave him a bear hug. My instincts were right, but I had no idea. Benjamin introduced us.

"These are my nephews Kyle and Eric, boys this is my good friend Briny *Spotted Owl* Stone he is of the Shoshone tribe we have known each other for many years."

We both shook his hands, but this was rather odd, How did Benjamin know when and where to stop or perhaps he didn't. This is just too coincidental there is nothing out here.

"Tell me how did you get the name spotted owl?"

Briny turned his back to us taking off his shirt, upon his back were of dark brown spots in the shape of feathers. His parents named him spotted owl because his marks are unique.

"Well it's very nice to meet you so tell me what you are doing out here?"

Briny pulled a cloth from his pocket wiping the sweat from his forehead.

Well young man I was waiting for your uncle, we have a lot of work to do. Briny told Benjamin the others were waiting on the next move. Many of them have been traveling all night and needed to get rest and food.

Benjamin said he would take Briny into town and drop him off at his hunting lodge where he could rest and get food. On the way there we Eric and I sat and listened while Briny updated Benjamin on what was happening. He told him how many more like us were disappearing and people were panicking.

Some taking their children and going underground, others reported seeing strange half man half wolf creatures in their dreams. Other reports were of a dark mist moving across the plains.

He told us that one night he was scouting near Snake River on his native land. He came across a group of hunters claiming to have spotted a huge wolf near their camp site. The men had guns and set traps, Briny encouraged the men to leave it was too dangerous, but the men did not listen him.

A wealthy business owner put up a twenty-thousand-dollar bounty for the capture of the huge wolves. Local authorities advised him to remove the bounty because it was just too dangerous. While Briny told the men to get off the land everything got quiet. No noise came from the woods only darkness and silence. He cautioned them not to make any sudden moves.

The hunters stood back to back of each with their guns drawn; Briny knew something was close by.

For the safety of the men and himself, Briny knew the Suhnoyee Wah would strike. Sensing his brothers nearby he telepathically spoke to them asking them to draw the Suhnoyee Wah away from him and the hunters.

That explains the sudden change in emotion with Benjamin, they were communicating with each other. He acted the same way when we rescued Nai'Okah. That was a very smart move on Briny's part. He continued to tell Benjamin on that night his brothers led the Suhnoyee Wah away from them he was able to convince the men that they did not belong there and should return home.

He told us many of our brothers and sisters were traveling further west to meet up with other tribes. A different breed of wolves was emerging, Benjamin asked what he meant by different breed. Briny said there are people who serve the Suhnoyee Wah thinking that they would be granted great power but only to be fooled. Once it has their blood it's all over until they transform.

Some do it just to serve evil allowing their bodies to be consumed, by summoning evil spirits to be used. They think they are invincible telling stories of how they can see things others can't. Eric cracked his knuckles.

"Trackers, we call them trackers. They turn on their own kind to serve evil, putting others at risk for the sake of others being killed."

Briny said he feared for the ones that have disappeared; the Suhnoyee Wah is killing anyone in the blood line. The more he talked the more my mind reflected on the night we rescued Nai'Okah, I prayed she was doing better. A tracker almost got her killed, with his evil worship of the Suhnoyee Wah.

Briny said many more natives from different tribes were still gathering the only way we can defeat the enemy is if everyone comes together. Tribal Elders have been overwhelmed with people arriving at the reservation to ask for blessings and protection.

Some are even performing blood rituals to see if they are direct descendants. Briny talked more about how tense things are and some people are even fleeing their native lands hoping to escape the dangers. He said many of them feel a great warrior will descend in the west to join in on the fight. He kind of looked over his shoulder at me when he said that. I asked him what he meant or who do the people say he or she is.

Briny explained.

There is talk amongst my people that there is a warrior reborn to appear in any form of his enemy. We call him *Muh Akicita* which means moon warrior. Our people believe that this warrior has the power of the moon to transform into his enemy to confuse him. This way the warrior can destroy the one he becomes. There are many legends, but stories have been told throughout generations that one day our people would be saved.

Eric also joined in on the conversation.

"Who do your people say it is? Are they male or female?"

Briny continued.

"We are not sure; the spirit guides choose many however there is talk amongst my people that the moon warrior will come from the west. Whoever he or she is I'm glad they're on our side."

We all agreed. Once we reached the lodge Benjamin told Briny to get a hold of the others and have them stay at the lodge. For a while, he would return shortly after he took us home. Briny said it was nice to meet us, and that we are very popular amongst our people. He said he was looking forward to meeting me again; there is a lot he could learn from me. I gazed at him.

He tapped the truck and walked away. By the time we arrived back home we had visitors. We went inside and to my surprise the visitors were Chief Morgan, Ms. Creed, Nai'jae and Dr. Morgan Elsha's dad. They were all sitting in the living room watching the news while Elsha was upstairs with the girls.

Chapter Nineteen

The Movement

"Hey everyone what's going on?"

Dad asked both of us to sit down; he told Benjamin it was always a pleasure seeing him again. Mom offered him a drink, but Benjamin said he couldn't stay long he had friends in town. Mom asked if it was a special occasion. Benjamin smiled at her then looked at me and Eric.

"No just a fishing expedition with some buddies of mine."

Dr. Morgan said he hadn't been fishing in years, Dad asked where he planned on going.

"So are you going any place close by?"

Benjamin shrugged his shoulders a little then he responded.

"No, no place in particular, just somewhere near Deer Creek.

Deer Creek is a popular fishing spot for the locals, the fish are pretty big. But then Chief Spearhorn warned Benjamin not to go there.

"Sorry to inform you my friend but the main road to the creek is closed. There have been wolf sightings in the area and we have cautioned the public to stay away until we can make sure it's safe. That's another reason why a few of us are here today we just want to be sure that everyone is safe."

Chief Morgan scratched his head and seemed very puzzled.

"The funny thing is some of the packs don't seem to impose a threat, but I have heard of other packs that are more aggressive. Same species different breed but anyway everyone needs to be safe."

Benjamin assured Chief Spearhorn that he was indeed going to be safe, but he may put off his fishing until things are clear. That was a great move on uncle's part, but I knew him and the others were going to do some investigating on their own.

Benjamin left for the lodge and I sat and talked with everyone for a while. Chief Spearhorn talked more about other packs of wolves being spotted at night so he wanted me and Eric to know that the curfew was still in place.

Elsha came down stairs with the girls, Becca and Nai'Jae embraced me with joy. They acted as if I was gone forever. Ms. Creed said she stopped by because Nai'Jae wanted to see me. She said she was doing much better now that she and Becca are friends.

With all the news reports our town is held prisoner by evil. Chief Morgan stressed to us again the importance of the curfew and children and pets should be monitored. Elsha talked about Boomer and Tango keeping her up at night with their barking. She has to stay at her uncle's house the nights her dad works late or when she babysits for mom and Ms. Creed.

Chief Spearhorn cautioned us not to go out past curfew and if we hear a noise do not go outside. Dad said he was taking me and Eric to the gun range a little later. But I was still curious why everyone was here. Something didn't seem right at all.

"Is there anything else going on that I should know about?"

Mom assured me everything was okay and there was no need to worry. Chief Morgan just wants all of us to be safe.

I didn't believe her, I looked over at dad and he lowered his eyebrows.

"Son, why don't you and Kyle meet me in the car I'll take you two to the gun range for a little target practice."

I told him I didn't feel like going I'd rather go some other day. Instead I decided to take the girls to the park Elsha and Eric joined me. The adults told us not to be gone long we told them we would be about an hour or less. The park wasn't far just a around the corner so there were no worries.

"What do you think is going on brother?"

I just sighed.

"I'm not sure."

But then Elsha told us what was really going on. While she was upstairs with the girls, she overheard her uncle talking about wolves traveling in packs through our state. She said there have been so many sightings of wolves traveling in packs. So far none have shown to be a threat to people, but her uncle is not taking any chances.

Something has got the animals stirred. Even they know what is coming. She told us how last night they had to bring the dogs in because they were barking too loud. Elsha said when they went outside it was dark and very quiet except for the dogs. She said the dog stared into the darkness and growled loudly.

She explained it was a strange night that even the horses started to get worked up. Elsha said it reminded her of the night she met that strange man. She covered her shoulders with her arms as if she was cold. Her dad told her to go inside with the dogs he would check on the horses.

Although Dr. Morgan didn't see anything, but she said her dad sure felt weird as if something or someone was watching.

Eric shivered again, his lips tightened; forming a fist he cracked his knuckles. I sensed my brother knew something. He asked Elsha did anything else strange happen that night. Elsha just told us that it took a while for the dogs to calm down, but Boomer and Tango never left her room. The dogs slept on the floor in front of her bed. Her dad deeply expressed to her she is not to stay at home alone when he is out of town.

Nothing else happened that night but her dad felt something else was going on until he got a phone call from Ms. Creed then from my mom about Becca. I was a little shocked something strange did happen but at separate households around the same time.

Apparently Nai'Jae had a nightmare and woke up screaming; when her mom couldn't calm her, she called for my dad. Not wanting Elsha to be left home alone he suggested she go with him.

Elsha talked about how both girls experienced the same nightmare. Each telling chilling details without knowing the others dream. We watched as both girls sat on the grass playing with their dolls. Eric said whatever they dreamed, they seemed be to be taking things well.

I could sense both girls were drawing strength from each other. As I watched them, they made a pact between them by locking their pinky fingers. I watched them for a few more minutes before deciding to approach them. I just had to know what deal they just made.

"Hey girls, having fun, what are you up to?"

Becca just smiled but I could tell she was still bothered by something.

"Nothing big brother were just talking."

I really wanted to know but they had been through enough already. Nai'Jae seemed to be doing okay she smiled at me a little. I could tell both girls were trying to be strong but neither one of them could bare it anymore. Eric and Elsha approached and gave the girls some assurance that they would be kept safe.

Both girls disagreed. Looking at each other with concerned looks they decided to tell us about their dreams. Both girls told us about seeing a war between good and evil. They even mentioned seeing the dark-skinned man with the blue eyes standing on top of a high mountain summoning the great elders.

As the night grew darker the eyes of the night shifters appeared watching and waiting. Revealing their long sharp teeth, they stepped forward from the darkness. The girls explained they were scary to look upon. As they watched painted warriors also appeared dressed for battle.

Moving toward each other the battle began, one by one the darkness swallowed them. Wolves of enormous size attacked the men from every side. Blood poured from the darkness staining the ground. Becca eyes began to tear up, I told her she didn't have to continue she was scared enough but then they both looked at each other Nai'Jae's voice trembled as she started to speak.

"A huge beast approached us and told us that we were already dead, and to give in to him, no one would come to our rescue, for in the dream we belonged to him. He has already tasted my blood; and now he wants my gift. He wants Becca's too."

She looked at us with teary eyes.

"You will protect me, won't you? Don't let him get to us please!"

She ran to me crying, putting her arms around me. Eric and Elsha comforted Becca. I told them that I would keep them both safe and Eric agreed. Then I suggested it would be a good Idea to get my family to safety far away from here.

Becca can't control what she sees just as we don't have control, it comes for a reason and sometimes we must embrace what we see and trust whatever causes us to see.

I asked Elsha if her mom was still requesting, she come for a visit. And she gave me a serious look.

"You're not thinking what I think you are right."

I wanted her to know how serious I was. I explained on the way back to the house.

"I think it would be a great idea for all of you to get as far away from here as you can. Call your mom and tell her you will take her up on her offer."

She didn't like the idea, but the odds were in my favor. By the time we had reached the house, there seem to have been more visitors and more talk of wolf packs. The movement was taking place I felt it ever so strong. Scores of them gathering preparing for war that was inevitable.

Chief Morgan was sending his wife Faith and the kids far into the next state. He suggested Elsha go with them, but she refused. Arguing with him, she was not having it. Neither was he, Ms. Creed was also sending Nai'Jae with Faith and the twins however Elsha felt backed into a corner. As her phone rang, she walked away to answer.

Chapter Twenty

MARKED

"Hey, mom."

I could tell she did not want to have this conversation. Elsha didn't want to disappoint her mother. She would do anything to stay.

"Elsha honey, I know this is a difficult time for you, but your dad and I talked and we think it is for the best you join us for while until things calm down."

Her hand gestures told me that the conversation did not go well. Her mom was in route to get her to take her away just for a while. The great thing about it is she will have mom, Becca and Nai'Jae with her along with her aunt Faith and the twins.

She just shook her head as she walked back toward us. She told me not to say anything.

"When do you leave?"

Elsha Just frowned.

"Few days, mom will be here to pick us up, well at least we get to ride in style she's sending a limo."

Well the girls seemed to be excited, except for Becca but Elsha said she would help her pack and promised she would keep her safe.

Back at the house Chief Morgan and I spoke while Elsha helped Becca pack her clothes. He told me he felt better if I were leaving too but he understood. He told me how fond Elsha was of me and he was glad that we are friends.

I mentioned how stubborn she can be at times and he just laughed, patted me on my shoulder and said he would feel better when our town felt safe again. I agreed.

Well the time came for everyone to leave; I wanted to spend time with Elsha before she left. I asked her to meet me at the park near my house. I know she didn't want to leave but I agreed with her dad and uncle she would be safer away from here.

"Thanks for meeting me, I wanted to thank you."

She looked at me with disappointment as we walked toward a secluded area.

"For what you said to Becca about taking care of her."

She responded.

"Yes of course."

I told her how much I appreciated her for all that she has done since we met. I really liked her and not knowing what was going to happen I felt she needed to know. Admiring her beauty, I felt my pulse rising. Elsha said I was sweating on forehead.

Her smell was ever so pleasant; I could hear the blood flowing through her veins. The sound of her heart beat was a music ensemble that soothed me. I could feel my chest enlarge so my palms were now sweating too.

I had to keep myself under control. The last time I felt like this strange things happened to me. I had to fight it off but for how long.

"Kyle is there something wrong your face is flushed."

I took a deep breath.

"Elsha, I just want you to know how much I appreciate our friendship, and I wanted to spend time with you before you left. I thought about how much we have been through together and..."

She stopped me.

"Wait, what? Are you asking me out? Kyle I am not ready for this. Look I value our friendship, but I just don't know if I'm ready for a relationship yet. Although I am flattered Kyle, but I just don't know. I care about you to, but can't this wait?

I didn't know what to feel or say, but however she was right, it is too soon. But I sensed something else.

"What are you afraid of?"

She was getting that agitated look again.

"Look around us Kyle too many things are happening, I don't want anything to happen to you."

I knew what she meant, we sat and talked for a few more minutes and then it was time for her to head to her uncle's house not before giving a long hug. With my arms around her she felt so good. I loved the smell her hair, the faint scent of perfume behind her ears, her soft skin. I didn't want to let go.

"Control yourself Kyle, control yourself."

But she didn't let go, she held on I mean really held on. Wow I held her until I could smell her blood, wait her blood? My breathing increased, I placed my hands on the back of her head and gripped her long black hair with my hand.

I leaned in closer and stared into her eyes. How I wanted to kiss her, but I respected her so much. My father taught me to always be respectful toward girls, so I gained control of myself.

She said she needed that and told me she got what she needed until she comes home.

But before we headed back, she planted one good one on me. Then she looked at me.

"This doesn't make us a couple until you return back home."

I was happy to hear that.

"Now you just gave me a reason to fight even harder."

It was time to for her to go to her uncle's, so she dropped me off at home. She said she would be back to pick up mom and Becca. When we got to the house Eric was outside.

He walked toward Elsha and spoke, she got out giving him a quick hug she thanked Eric for being a good friend. She told him to make sure he came back home as well.

After she left Kyle just stared at me.

"What is that look for?"

He smiled.

"What were you two up to did something happen?"

I played innocent.

"Just talk, nothing else."

Eric was not buying it all he knew the truth after all he was my twin.

"Dude your scent was all over her, I mean it's embedded. Look at yourself, your bigger than you were before you left."

I knew something was going on other than my hormones racing. I explained to him what happened and how my breathing got heavy, and the smell of Elsha's blood. He told me whatever I did I marked her somehow. He laughed and called me a bloodhound. He said I would be able to find her anywhere now.

I just shook my head.

"Wait you mean I imprinted on her that cant' be real like dude that is the movies, right?"

He just stared at me.

"Well kind of, if your body goes through changes while in the presence of a female you like. You can mark them by what you release like a signal to others that she's taken in a way."

Now I was really laughing.

"That is the craziest thing I'd ever heard, you must be joking."

Eric just looked at me.

"You will see brother you will see."

We walked into the house mom and the girls were pre-packing their suitcases. Mom had that worried look in her eye, but I told her we would be okay. We took the suitcases out to the garage then she went to prepare dinner.

Chapter Twenty One

Past Reflections

The day has finally come. My mind goes back to when this all started, and now all I want is for this to end. No more deaths, my fight is with an ancient warrior that betrayed his own kind. He has slaughtered countless, men women and children for centuries. It was time for the nightmare of all nightmares to finally come to an end.

My mind reflected on how peaceful this town once was. Fear has polluted towns everywhere, paralyzed even the strongest, and the weak trembled. But then there is us, a different breed, not like anyone else, chosen to defend those who can't defend themselves.

The foul stench of traitors was everywhere; I prepared myself for this day not knowing if I would ever see my family again it was our duty to restore that peace that was taken away.

At the gun range, dad had us getting ready for target practice. We were in one of the secluded areas where you must have special clearance to get more of a longer range. The targets were covered up but before dad removed them, he gave us a heart to heart talk.

"I know you boys have a destiny that I do not understand. Son I almost lost you once and I will not lose you again. TThere are things going on that I will never understand, be able to explain. I know it has something to do with both of you. So that is why I want to give you a reason to come back home to all us."

Dad uncovered, the targets to reveal a dark image on the canvas. It was the same image that was on the camera outside of our home.

I didn't understand why dad would show us this; I know he didn't believe anything before, but the death of his friend and the drawings was proof enough for him, I guess.

"I believe whoever this person is killed my friend Mike, whatever he saw scared him to death. His wife said he saw images in his dreams until they became real. Son I never told you this, but his wife found images, sketched in books she found. I asked her to give them to me so I'm giving them to you make sure Chief Spearhorn gets it. He's taking you two to Wyoming, although I am against it but I would rather you be far way from here as possible. I now know that whatever was after my friend must be after either you or Becca."

We must have shot at that target over a thousand times; the image was imbedded in my head. Dad kept telling us to focus and don't miss. We are at it for hours, then I stopped, something caught my eye just over the ridge from where we were shooting. Eric noticed as well.

"See something out there bro?"

I didn't move nor even blinked, slowly adjusting the scope on the rifle to look for signs of movement. Dad was on the lookout as well. Then we spotted them, had to be at least seven or more herds of deer.

"Just looking at the herds moving, they don't seem to be startled but they are on the move."

We watched for awhile making sure predators were not following them, dad gave the all clear. But I didn't think so; I kept feeling as if we were being watched. I looked over my shoulder and stared at the ridge. If something was up there is was very still. My impulse was kicking in but I knew we had to get back. Mom and the girls will be leaving soon, and I wanted to make sure Elsha was not trying to pull any type of escape.

It was a nice drive back at home, but I couldn't help the feeling I had. Time was drawing closer for us to leave with Chief Spearhorn. We explained to dad how big this event was, and how Natives from all over the world meet up at Devils Tower. Knowing that they are far away from here now made me feel better it had to be this way. Many ceremonies take place there Chief Spearhorn this is the time of year where past meet present. Each tribe comes with their own history and traditional stories all very similar. This is the way we reserve our American Indian culture.

As we arrive back at the house a long stretch Limo was parked out front along with Police Chief Morgan, Elsha's dad and mom. They greeted us as we approached the house, Dr. Morgan introduced us

"Hello Tom, boys I'd like to introduce you to Elsha's mom Denise."

However, she was just a bit too anxious to meet me, but she had to tell me and Eric apart first.

"Oh, my you do look alike, which one of you is Kyle?"

This was awkward, but now I know where Elsha gets those pretty eyes from. Her mother was drop dead gorgeous.

"I'm Kyle ma'am this is my twin brother Eric."

She was an amazing woman.

"Well it's nice to meet you both; will you be joining us as well? You know you are welcome to come, with all of the scary things going on around here this town just doesn't seem safe anymore."

Dr. Morgan joined in on the conversation.

"Denise, this is Tom, Kyle's father and his mother Helen is inside with the girls."

Denise and dad shook hands; well at least the welcome was a warm one. The chauffer assisted with the luggage as everyone came outside. It was a bitter sweet moment, but it was for the best Mom, Becca, Nai'jae, and Elsha would be better off. Although the Suhnoyee Wah could appear anywhere at any time, but deep within I felt the girls would be safe.

Becca was nervous about going but she was more afraid for me. The look she had in her eyes was a sure sign of it. She ran and jumped in my arms and squeezed me tight.

"I will be praying my brother, but I want you to know there are more on your side than you know. But promise me you will return back home."

I gave her all the assurance she needed to hear, she didn't need to worry about me my I know what I needed to do. I just had to for her sake; Becca was such a unique little girl with a remarkable gift. But she shouldn't have to live her life in fear; I had to put an end to this madness.

Looking around at everyone, I knew time was drawing near for me to face my destiny. After we said our goodbyes, it was time for Eric and I to get going as well Chief Spearhorn and Big John would be arriving soon. My mind reflected on the past thinking about all that I have been through. It's not something that is easy. I spent half my life running from something I did not understand, but now that I know I am not alone although I am still haunted and hunted.

I am not sure if my nightmare will ever end, or if this war will be the end of me. I see myself as that little boy laying on the table strapped, while the dark entity hovered over me.

No one could see it but me, trying to explain something to someone that only you can see is not something you want to tell. I learned to embrace what I am, although I don't think I have touched the surface of it yet.

I feel crazy, but I know I am not; I'm just different with a little extra gift. I would have never known what I was destined to do if my nightmares never started. Getting help from someone like Ms. Creed to make you feel sane of instead of insane. I have important people in my life that help me fight this battle. It felt good knowing that I was never alone, although I felt like I was.

Meeting Tony, Elsha, my twin brother Eric, Big John my uncle Benjamin, my family circle grew along with my strength. Family is important; the strength of a family can defeat anything that rises against it. We can face many things alone, but together face it as one.

That thought stuck with me, I repeated it over and over in my head. After I packed my suitcase, Big John and Chief Spearhorn arrived, I had never been to Devils Tower, but I have read the stories in text books. But even they sometimes don't give the full truth unless you sit with tribal elders and hear them brought to life right before you. I was excited about going; Eric was too, I think he packed more food than clothes.

Dad just laughed at him, he wanted to be sure we had what we needed and said that it would be good for us to go and experience our native culture. He said it would be best, I wasn't comfortable with dad staying but he said he was going to be with Police Chief Morgan. Strange things were still happening, but I felt it was moving due west.

Something was definitely coming, and it was big. This gathering that was taking place and the wolf sighting in great numbers. People who study animal behaviors are even puzzled. Some are even saying it is the sign of the times. Before disaster strikes, the animals flee.

But I beg to differ, with Elsha's mom Denise, taking everyone, I prayed for their safety. Knowing that they are far away from here now made me feel better it had to be this way. Big John and Chief Spearhorn thanked dad for allowing us to travel with them. At first dad and Chief Spearhorn did not see eye to eye concerning me when I was near death. Time made up for that.

Chief Spearhorn gave dad a pouch filled with healing herbs, and a blanket. He shared a few kind words of wisdom dad also stated he wanted us to keep safe and he would see us when we got back and then we were on our way.

We had a few days drive, but it would be a good one, we met up with a few others and we were on our way. Chief Spearhorn was very quiet and I could hear him mumble a few silent prayers from his lips. I'm not sure what was going on but this side of him I have never seen. It seems he was in deep meditation.

Chapter Twenty Two

BORN IN THE BLOOD

Once we arrived in Wyoming, we settled in on the camp grounds where giant teepees were setup everywhere. Each one representing tribes from every nation. Some were draped in symbols, colors of red, yellow, turquoise, and many other colors. Booths were also setup with memorabilia of Native American art and paintings. For generations they have gathered to tell stories keeping the traditions alive.

There was a huge platform, decorated with flags and tribal banners. The huge rock was the back drop which made everything seemed so perfect. Most of the elders were already in place, many things caught my attention, and strange symbols like the ones from my dream outlined one of the teepees. These were the ones I saw painted on the dark-skinned man with the crystal blue eyes. I could feel a strong sense of power coming from it.

The few days we have spent here have been great so far. It was such an experience meeting other brother and sisters from different tribes. There were scores of them all over the place, Meeting people from all parts of the globe sharing stories. I can say it was very nice to see some familiar faces from the reservation. Dr. Gregory Spears and, Nurse Mei'omi were there as well. He told me it was good to see me. I responded by telling him the same.

He asked if he could speak with me alone for a moment, so we took a walk. We talked mostly about my time spent in the hospital. He said he saw many patience, but I was his most peculiar patient. He asked if anyone ever told me about my blood, I said yes, somewhat. He said the night I was brought into the hospital I had lost a lot of blood. He said the good thing was my donor was an exact match and that I was born in the blood line. I asked him what that meant.

He said being born in the blood line says a lot although my blood was different. I also wondered why Elsha's dad took an interest in my blood as well. Dr. Spears stated that my blood is strong and when blended with my brothers it becomes more powerful.

Dr. Spears continued.

"We lost you several times, and brought you back by using your brother's blood, when we mixed it, it not only rejuvenated you, but you seem to heal a lot faster. We also notice how your blood increased your muscle mass. Many things began to happen to you. You body went through changes, that we did not allow anyone near you. We know how to take care of our own kind, so you had to come to us."

Then he flexed his muscles, laughed, and punched me in the arm.

"You are a blood descendant of the Spearhorns, you are definitely chosen to be in the blood line, look at your uncles Big John and Benjamin."

I laughed again at him. I was grateful for how they took good care of me though.

He told me how unique I was, and to embrace my gift, because it is a powerful one and that we all must be careful. I agreed, he said he would see me a little later he had a few things to put together. I do remember them saying my blood type was different. I know that now because of the things that have been happening to me.

As I headed back to meet with Eric and the others, looking around at everything, it reminded me of when I first met Benjamin, that night I was chased right into his tent. I remember seeing all the crystals and things he had that night. I was chased but ushered to his tent. Something guided me to him. They have always been with me, my parents, and the dark-skinned man with the crystal blue eyes. The white mist, I was never alone.

Then I felt a strong presence, it was Becca, I searched my thoughts. I couldn't call her because there was not much cell phone service. Perhaps if I could get somewhere with good reception, I could call her. I decided to walk to one of the ridges to see if I could get a signal. But my attention was driven into another direction. A few men were watching the stars, and others were staring into the darkness.

But there was something else that caught my attention. The smell of war there was no way I could shake it. It was in the air like a skunk releasing its toxic spray. I walked toward a big huge rock; the other Elders were up front waiting for Chief Spearhorn to join them. They began to setup more bonfires; several men were dressed up like warriors standing on either side of the stage. The moon appeared so close to the earth you could reach out and touch it.

Eric joined me along with Big John, Spotted Owl, and Benjamin. We stood next to each other watching the elders. Chief raised his eagle head staff in the air as a sign of silence. He addressed the crowds of people and began to tell them how important it was for everyone to come together.

"An enemy of our past has come to disrupt our future. We must stand together to protect our lineage. The forces of evil are upon us. This is a time of for us as a people to come together; we have lost so many to this evil. The moon is close to earth as foretold centuries ago, our people have suffered a great loss, but we will not let this stop us for the time has come for us to prepare ourselves and stop this evil one."

As we stood listening Chief Spearhorn spoke very strong about our native culture. He said that we should embrace each other and hold on to our beliefs. He spoke about how the ancients sent out sacred prayers to protect our people from the Suhnoyee Wah. The survival of our people is very important; together we will stand together no matter what it takes.

Many thoughts ran though my mind while I sat and listened to the elders speak. What they lived through, and how they survived it. Their seasoned years of wisdom must be preserved. They are my history, just as much as we are their future. Now I understand how much our elders are needed. They are the decorative jewels that shine deep within us. We need them as much as they need us to survive.

After the opening speech ceremony of the tribal elders, some returned to their Teepee Huts, while others were scouting the land. My brother and I decided to join a few others at the bonfires to dance under the moon. I also couldn't help to think about my family and I prayed for their safety. I thought of Elsha and wondered if she was doing okay as well. I know she would have wanted to be here, but this was no place for her.

Past and present coming together under a giant moon I could feel their strength and energy. As we prepared our garments, we met a young woman named Anai'lique, she had the look of a fierce warrior, she stood tall, and walked with authority. She too was joining us in the dance. We learned she is from the Catawba Tribe they called themselves *yeh is-WAH h'reh*, meaning "people of the river."

Along with others we took our place, the drummers were in position then the dancing started, but this was no ordinary dance, this was dance of victory. The elders spoke of this during the ceremony that any time before a war the tribes would dance and sing. With everyone coming together believing in a victory, it gave the tribe great strength in knowing their battle was already won.

We danced, praised, and sang tribal songs. Others sat telling ancient stories, and others sold artifacts. It was a good night underneath the moon, I swear at times it was getting closer and closer to the earth. Then it dawned on me, when the earth touches the sky, I kept whispering that to myself. Deep down I knew what that meant, I'm sure others knew it to.

At the end of the dance another tribal elder from a distance tribe, represented the Shoshone tribe his name was Chief William Modoc as he took to the podium.

He spoke words of war, vowing to uphold the tradition of keeping the lives of our past loved ones alive. He spoke on those that vowed to put an end to the evil that has struck fear in the hearts of our people. He vowed that the nightmare would end; it was time to cleanse our hearts and minds. He said we needed to become one with the ancestors remembering those who lost their lives. Then all the elders stood together on the podium to mark the start of the ceremony. Just as their staffs were raised the diamonds in eyes of the eagle head glowed brightly.

The fires cracked in the dark crisp night. An eerie wind blew across the plain the elders stood closer, tighter each one holding up their staffs as the silver stones lit up inside them.

Then I felt a change taking place within me. A heightened sense of smell almost caused me to shift right out of my skin. Something or someone was getting closer. Benjamin and Big John both looked at me. I nodded, Eric and Spotted Owl stood firm. Others soon joined I wasn't the only one feeling a change.

A slight wind blew an all too familiar smell again. My body swelled until my clothes tightened

There was no time but to act. Screams rang out in the distance, and then more screams. Looking around all I could see was a dark mist moving, Lights from the silver stones could barely brake through. I could hear Eric, but I couldn't see him.

"Eric, where are you! Brother, can you hear me!"

He quickly responded.

"Yes, I'm here, it's time to blend in brother, stay close!"

We stood ground as the shifters moved all around us. A band of White and grey wolves were now in the place where the Chief Elders once stood. But we could no longer see them, but their stones were still glowing. Then out from the darkness something stepped forward. Others soon followed you can't fight an enemy you can't see but when you draw him out of his element you can weaken him for the kill.

With the others close by my side I moved in closer. Eric gripped his knife tightly I could hear his knuckles crack. We must get to the Elders but being immediately surrounded we knew it was time to fight. Benjamin told Eric to pave the way then he took the crushed powder out of his bag and tossed it quickly in to the air.

We could see more Elders ahead of us surrounded, each one standing with their backs toward each other. If they can start with the strong and kill them, the weak will be left at their mercy. I was not going to let that happen. One by one they emerged as if stepping through a portal, revealing their claws and teeth.

But the beast I wanted had not yet revealed himself, I had to get closer; Spotted Owl was ahead of me then out of the darkness a beast lunged at him, but his fighting skills were remarkable. We could not stop, fighting our way through. Others joined in with us, some snatched by huge claws reaching out of the darkness.

We were getting closer, but not close enough, the Elders were holding ground, keeping the shifters away with the silver stones, but the closer they moved in on them the light revealed their true form which allowed our fellow brothers and sisters to destroy them.

I've never seen such fighting abilities like this before, but I'm glad they are on our side. There were many of us but more of them, then what sounded like an explosion, halted everyone, it was as if someone through a lightning bolt in the mist of the camp. Light was everywhere, now I did not know for how long, but it bought us time to reach the Elders.

Then he appeared just as he did in my dreams, the man that I had been seeing was now visible to me in plain sight.

"Am I dreaming or are you really here?"

He smiled and nodded.

Chapter Twenty Three

THE BLOOD POOL

"I am very real."

I was no longer dreaming, he was very real and ready for war. He had saved my life so many times; some have said this man was a myth. Other say he was chosen by the spirit guides to walk the earth to protect the chosen ones. Whatever he just did sent the Suhnoye Wah back into the darkness.

Standing face to face to face with him, it was as if time stood still. No shifters were in sight, but the damage was already done, blood stained the ground. The wounded were taken to a nearby tent to be cared for.

Eric and the others joined me. The dark-skinned man told us that we were the key to end the nightmare of all nightmares. He said he only stopped them for a moment, but they would return. The four elders still standing with their backs to each other stood under the huge moon. They did not move but seemed to be in a trance. Huge gray and white wolves guarded them.

This was happening all too fast, he told me to keep my mind clear, and watch for anything different in the night. He told us to watch with careful eyes.

He took his thumb and placed it on my forehead, leaving a dark smudge mark. He even did the same to Erica and the others. He spoke to us and gave us a weapon to use. He gave others sharp spears to use against them.

"Watch for a ripple in the darkness, when you see if move that is when you strike, take these and keep them on you they are small but very powerful."

The sharp stones he gave us were made of pure silver and diamond dust. He said when the night moves throw it and watch the shifter change form. Once it is revealed throw the spear and pierce the heart, this will destroy them, but they move fast and more will come. He told Benjamin to gather more men and set them on watch, the elders had to be guarded. The wolves on the stage did not move either, but they sniffed the air, and growled. Watching their surroundings, I knew Chief Spearhorn was in there, he and the others were heavily guarded now by these protectors. Other warriors joined with us as we prepared for battle.

The Legend of the Suhnoyee Wah goes back centuries when the Elders burned Liwanu alive. As he was dying, he vowed to get revenge on every generation connected to the tribal elders from each tribe. And for centuries many have vowed to protect us, and many have died saving us. As more and more of our people arrived, they had just walked into a war zone, word had spread fast. One of them kneeled to the blood-stained ground. He dipped his finger in it tasting it, then quickly he spits on the ground, he removed a decorative powder horn from his hip and poured the dark powder in the blood pool.

I had never seen this before. I watched carefully as others did the same thing. As soon as the dark powder was poured on the blood, it disappeared. I asked why this was done, and then Anai'lique approached.

"This stops the scavengers from coming, if they taste the blood on the ground, they can track the victims. My tribe also uses the powder, it keeps more than the scavengers away."

I was not surprised to hear this, but I wanted to know what she meant by that. But as I asked her screams were coming from the medical tent where Dr. Spears was.

Anai'lique, slowly drew an arrow from the bow case on her back, dipping the spearhead in the black powder. Then a man came running out from one of the tents, eyes black as night. He sniffed the air and ground, and when he saw her, he charged at her in full beast mode. Anai'lique didn't move she aimed and just when the man was in close range, she released the arrow striking the man in his chest.

He hit the ground with such a force, she looked over at me with her fearless eyes.

"This is why we put the powder in the blood pool, when one of ours is turning they can't hunt or track us. Keep your eyes open, and stay ready, I would expect you to do the same thing to me before it's too late."

Dr. Spears and the others crowded around the man taking him back to the tent. He said the arrow barely missed his heart, but he would live. Dr. Spears examined his eyes and they returned to normal. I wondered why he didn't die, I walked toward to the tent, but Benjamin stopped us. We were told to let them handle it.

Others were scouting and keeping watch. The dark-skinned man was preparing war paint as Spotted Owl gave us an update on the perimeters. He said everything appeared to be okay, for now but the elders have not moved. Still heavily guarded, no one could get near them. The protectors are here for a reason that we all know about. More and more people arrived but I couldn't help but think about my family. I needed to talk to them.

I asked Benjamin if he could get a signal and he said he couldn't. I didn't like this at all but I needed to keep my focus. More bonfires were started as other Natives took their places, Dr. Spears came and gave us and update on the man Anai'lique shot with her arrow, he gave it back to her stating whatever it was coated with saved his life.

He asked if she mind sharing. Anai'lique took a pouch from her bag and gave it to Dr. Spears, she said he father gave her a special powder mixed with diamond dust from the silver stones. She said her father was a medicine man back home on the reservation. He made many healing potions and powders for protection. I asked her if she knew the man would survive and she said he would. She told us how her people used special powders to protect their land from predators.

She told us one winter her brother Saiben went hunting in the forest and didn't come back. Her father and the other men searched the forest for days looking for him. There was no sign of him anywhere, but her father never gave up hope. They searched night and day until they found him lying unconscious in a blood pool. He had a wound on his arm and at first, they didn't know what caused it.

There was no time, a storm was approaching so they had to seek shelter. Acting fast they dug holes in the ground to protect themselves while others built a sweat lodge. Anai'lique told us how the men placed Saiben in the sweat lodge to start the purification process. They didn't know how much blood he had lost but when they undressed him, he had been bitten several times. His body was full of fever and knew he was dying.

Her father began the cleansing of his blood, and then mixed the dark powder and crushed diamond stones covering him from head to toe. He drew sacred prayers on his body, then wrapped him in white cloths.

They covered the lodge with blankets and heated rocks, the winds ripped fierce that night all they could do was wait. Loud screams came from within the lodge but there was not much they could do. Anai'lique told us how she was able to follow her father, after the storm had past. When she saw her brother emerge from the lodge, but he looked different. He charged at the men, until he saw her, she said he had the same look in his eyes as the man she shot with her arrow tonight.

She said she knew that was not her brother, she reached behind her and drew her arrow, and shot, she missed the first one, then she drew another and missed again. Still charging at her, she could here her father yelling at her. But she ignored him, something in her told her to pierce from within, on the third try she shot the arrow striking him in his chest. Saiben lay lifeless in the snow. His blood turned the white snow black, not red.

They stood and watch while her father turned him over and broke the arrow, they carried him back to the reservation and watched him for a few days. Anai'lique told her story without emotion, her story of the Suhnoyee Wah was not like others I have heard but very similar. She knew that was not her brother, just as she knew the man was not himself. The arrow was more than just a healing potion, it was poisonous, if mixed just right the poison can cleanse the infected person from the inside out.

It is very dangerous, but it worked. Her brother was cleansed, but the blood of whatever bit him was still there. She says her brother has no memory of what happened to him in the woods only that he was attacked by something he couldn't see. Only that she knew adding the poison to the mix would work. When asked how she knew that from Dr. Spears, she explained a visitor had stopped by the reservation looking for her father to offer help by sharing healing potions.

Since her father was not there, he showed her how to mix it with poison blackberries. The man explained adding too much could kill, but just one drop would work against the poisoned blood.

Who would have thought fighting poison with poison, but it worked. Dr. Spears asked Anai'lique to assist him, this could help save more lives before it is too late. He asked her if there was another way, but she said it must pierce from the outside.

He also inquired about needle injections she said it just might work but it could be very dangerous. Anai'lique mentioned there was something else, if the injection is not given in enough time, you will have to make the kill without hesitation.

Dr. Spears agreed, nurse Meo'mi stopped by to inform us the patient is doing better. She looked at Anai'lique

"Whatever you did back there thank you, the man you saved was my brother."

Ana'lique was grateful.

"Your welcome, I did what I had to do. We have lost too many of our people, now we can save them."

As they left to go attend to him, word spread throughout the camps, everyone started to come together even more. Although panic and fear were having its way, many remained strong. Cleansing their minds, not allowing anything to distract them.

I wanted to talk to my parents to let them know I was okay. I'm glad they are safe and far away from harm I pray at least.

The moon appeared bigger and brighter, you could reach out and touch it. Upon the high mound I could see the dark-skinned man with his arms raised holding two staffs in each hand. I had a gut feeling something was about to change and fast.

I needed to get to Chief Spearhorn, but the elders were heavily guarded. I located my uncle and brother. Benjamin and Big John sensed it too, he told me it was time. We needed to connect, join as one tribe.

He said to clear our minds. Others joined as we stood in front of the fire. One of the men threw a white powder in the air above the fire we watched as the flames grew. A giant wall of surrounded us, creating a giant barrier.

The Chief Elders appeared before us, speaking almost simultaneously, great light surrounded them.

"Join with us now and prepare for great battle. The time has come the Suhnoyee Wah will bring unspeakable forces, keep your eyes and ears sharp, combine your strength and strike back against them."

Just as they were finished, and the flames disappeared, we each knew what to do. I ran to my tent, I could hear Eric calling out to me. I didn't look back. I needed to retrieve my bag I don't know why I needed it, somehow within I knew the ancient head piece holds the key. No more gut instincts, now it's just knowing. When I reached the tent, my entrance was blocked by a huge beast, there was no time for hesitation. It stood tall, growling, and snarling at me.

Chapter Twenty Four

THE GREAT WAR

I must get inside this beast or any other was not going to stop me. Staring the beast eye to eye, I slowly withdrew my knife holding steady I was ready, then Eric joined me just as the beast lunged forward.

An arrow flew between us striking it in the middle of its forehead, I didn't wait to turn around to see who shot it. I struck the beast across the neck, while Eric stabbed it, we fought the beast to its end. We turned to see Anai'lique standing behind us. I entered the tent to retrieve my bag, I had to hurry before others appeared. Eric told me as soon as I took off, he saw a dark shadow follow me. Anai'lique also saw it and kept her arrow steady. But she wanted to know what I was up to.

"What is in that bag that you need so much? Is your life worth it?"

I quickly responded.

"This is more than just about me, it's about all of us. We kill the main beast, we kill the rest. But first we must force him out into human form. The smell of burnt flesh will tell us when he is near."

Eric also commented.

"Beast or human we must kill it, too many of our people have died, it stops tonight. Whether we live or die we must fight with everything we got,"

Opening my bag, I placed the ancient headdress on my head. Anai'lique added the war paint but this paint sparkled. She said she used powder from the silver stones, as she placed it on my arms and face, they began to tattoo like magic. I asked her if it was supposed to burn and she said no.

She told me it was a sure sign, that we were chosen for this day. But it was evident enough a transformation was taking place, my arms and legs increased in muscle mass. Ana'lique also applied the war paint to Eric, he also changed a little. Stepping away from us she began to reveal more.

"I have heard stories of two twin boys that share an ancient power, I never thought I would see it or witness it firsthand. Yet human you have shifting capabilities, the dark matter in your eyes tell me you are part beast. I heard of your attack when you and Elsha went missing. That night when you were attacked by the wolf. My father told me he was there. As your blood drained into the ground, he waited until everyone left and collected as much as he could. He used diamond powder to dry up what was left. He did this to throw off the scent of trackers, my father found a way to use your blood in his healing potions. A few of my arrows are dipped in that same potion, I can't do this alone, but I will try to save as many as I can." Some of my brothers and sister are already here, hiding, waiting to strike. We will cover your both."

There was no time to go into further details, we had to get moving. The others met up with us as we took our places. I did not know when or where the next strike would take place. The brighter the moon the more ancient tattoos appeared. As we walked toward the open valley, some were snatched by the darkness. Screams rang out in the night; the war had begun. Shifters were making their appearance.

Uncle Benjamin and Big John transformed into monstrous beasts, walking along side of us, and arrow shot right above us into the darkness as a beast fell to the ground wounded. Others pounced on the beast killing it. The smell of burnt flesh began to fill the air. Eric stayed close by my side.

Anai'lique and the others took their positions, I told her to keep the arrows in the air as it will mark the beast's whereabouts. Still guarded by the ancient wolves they defended the elders, I didn't know what they were waiting for. Flaming arrows filled the night sky as they revealed the Suhnoyee Wah, warriors launched themselves into the dark matter, some returned while others did not.

Blood spilled all over the ground, we fought for what seemed like hours until everything got quiet. Not one sound was made, dead silence was everywhere. I told everyone to keep still. Then it happened, the horrific sounds, the smell of burnt flesh. Dark matter moved across the night sky it was as if a portal was opening from another dimension, I knew this day would come. A white misty fog moved above the covering the blood on the ground. Silhouettes of ghostly images also appeared.

Eric moved in closer drawing his knife. I could feel his adrenaline increasing.

I softly whispered to him.

"Not yet my brother, wait."

One of the wolves moved in between us, the other packs also joined us. Other wolves also growled showing strength. A huge white wolf also stood next to me, I didn't have time to think about anything all I knew was this beast had to die.

Dark matter surrounded us like a thick blanket. A white wolf stood tall, facing the dark entity growling as its claws grew increasingly long. For a moment you would think it was driving the beast back into the dark matter. The white wolf turned facing us, it stared me deep into my eyes, I could sense it was one of the chief elders.

His gestures urged us to move back. He spoke to me telling me more were coming, but before he could do anything else claws tore right through him. Right before us a huge beast emerged from the darkness, growling revealing its sharp teeth. As the white wolf fell to the ground, it howled in agony. A fast-moving white mist quickly covered it.

A great one has fallen right before me, the sound it made was an alarm sending others running towards our direction. Eric charged him with great anger. Prepared for battle we were once again fighting but not for us, for life, for our families, and for the generations to come. Just as my ancestors did during their time of wars.

Many lost their lives while others were saving lives. If we are not afraid to die, then we can't be afraid to live. But if we are not successful, I pray the living keep on fighting until this evil has been wiped off the face of the earth. The night sparkled with arrows as they were shot from the trees, as we now know we must end this to stop the beast that has vowed to destroy us. Eric and I fought back to back and watched as they came for us one by one.

The more they charged at us we charged at them, I kept my eyes sharpened as the one beast that vowed to kill me was moving in and out of the darkness. When fighting this evil one must become it or draw it out into its true form. I told my brother to watch my move, on the count of three to toss the crystal powder into the air.

Eric held steady then one, two, three, he threw the powder into the air, and we simultaneously struck the beast. As it changed before us, we continued to strike for the kill. The beast known as Liwanu, was changing into human form. For a moment he vanished into the darkness only to return and snatch Eric. I couldn't believe what was happening before my eyes I screamed.

"Eric, Eric!

I could see him fighting back as he called out to me.

"Brother, no stay back, stay back!

Then he was gone, I acted quickly, Anai'Lique rushed to my side as the human face of Liwanu appeared.

"Where is he, what happened?"

There was no time to explain, I knew what had to be done next. I could hear my brother screaming. Then he appeared again holding my brother by the neck, I could see Eric fighting him. With each count I timed the appearance and reappearance of my brother.

"You want him, then come get him!"

"Anai'Lique said in a still small voice as she aimed her arrows"

"No problem."

Before she released them into the darkness she said.

"Cut yourself, I need your blood, do it now!"

I didn't hesitate, I pulled out my knife cutting my hand, I cuffed my hand to keep the blood from spilling out, then she dipped the arrowhead in my palm coating it with my blood. She said to take the remainder and pour it into a small bottle attached to her hip.

She closed her eyes and focused on Eric's voice she whispered an ancient language then she shot her arrows through the dark matter.

Growls and screams were everywhere, I watched as a human figure leaped out of the darkness onto the ground. He had his head down, breathing heavy. I started to approach him but Anai'Lique grabbed my arm and told me to wait. Anai'Lique prepared another arrow. I called out to Eric. Others stood with knives and other weapons just in case.

"Eric, my brother, Are you with us!"

Then he stood waiving his hands as a sure sign, he just needed a moment to catch his breath. Benjamin and Big John told everyone to lower their weapons, but Anai'Lique did not, she never took her eyes off him.

"We need to be sure he is your brother, there is a pouch around my neck with a small vial inside, take it and make him drink it. Then I will lower my arrows."

With her arrows aimed at his chest, Benjamin and Big John made sure Eric was still one of us by giving him the potion to drink. Of course, he was being himself by making choking gestures as if he was changing, but he was joking.

after getting a mouth full of Anai'Lique's potion I was glad to see he was telling the truth and I was glad to have my brother back. Others were not so lucky. The moon was getting closer there was not much time. We need to draw the beast out into human form, but I was not sure how we could do that, this beast was toying with us.

We reached the giant wolves and was greeted by one of them that blocked my way. I just shouted at them, until one of them growled at me in my face, I didn't move at all. No show of fear, no emotion. From deep within I let out a large growl while facing the guardian wolf. A voice spoke from beyond them and they allowed us to pass.

Once inside we were met by ghostly figures of men and women in ancient attire. They explained they are also fighting along with us.

"As the moon draws nearer, we all needed to combine our strength now. The beast within Liwanu is growing stronger every minute, we must remain in this state to protect the living. We along with the others have joined in the fight to end this battle with the Suhnoyee Wah. The evil it has done must now be forever cleansed from the earth."

War also must be won in the outer realms, they were reading our thoughts answering our questions even before we spoke a word. I wanted all of this to end, I wanted it to be over and go home to my parents. The more I thought about Becca, Ms. Creed, and Nai'Jae the angrier I became.

Not seeing my parents or my friends again would also be devasting, but this is not my end, it's the end of what has been haunting me and my people for centuries. Why should I allow something that once had a conscious heart to devour me because of the foolish mistakes it made long ago? This is my life and I will no longer live in fear! It is time to end this now! We have already joined our forces together. But a familiar voice spoke to me.

"Not all of us son, we are here with you together."

The voice of my mother comforted me.

"When all descendants arrive then the circle will be complete. Then we join all of us together."

That's it, all joined and others merge.

Liwanu died by fire in front of the Elders circle, I asked everyone to grab what they could to build a bonfire, Spotting owl, Big John and Benjamin prepared the others. Each tribe gathered in a circle facing opposite representing the four corners of the earth, a trench was dug to pour water around the fire, totem polls were coated in crushed diamond powder.

Torches were also lit, there was no time for speeches, no time for words at all. Eric described to me what it was like when he was grabbed, he said he could feel his life being sucked from him, but also someone was trying to pull him out.

He witnessed others devoured by the night, but he kept fighting. It was like being in a deep sleep fighting to wake up. This beast has plagued our dreams, now it is time we plagued his with ours.

Just as we were finished, the fire was big enough to be seen from miles away, some of the women used blankets to send out a signal, which glistened in the night sky. Scores of tribes also arrived, along with two familiar faces. Tilileah, and Milileah had arrived. Other descendants of the tribal elders that had once done away with Liwanu traveled to put and end to the evil as well. Just as their fathers once stood, they too now stand with us.

Both women called for me and my brother Eric to come forward. They each took small decorated staffs with feathers and waved them over us. Tilileah placed a war headdress on Eric's head, with a huge red stone in the center. Their eyes were changing colors and they sang in high pitch, dancers and drummers took their places. It seemed as if we were traveling back in time. I could see ancient warriors standing in position ready for war.

The women took their places with the others singing, while others danced and played drums. The chief Elders also joined us, dressed in battle gear. Chief Spearhorn was among them as well. This is déjà vu all over again. The night became still, and quiet. My brother and I stood back to back I watched as the dark matter moved again, then from out of the darkness.

Ancient tattoos sparkled like diamonds all over me, Liwanu wanted more than just revenge, he wanted to rule both realms, he wanted it all so much that he offered himself to the darkness of evil. Perhaps it was more than just Liwanu, but the evil that men seek from the other side to obtain power from their own ambitious ways.

It is more than just Liwanu we are fighting, it is an evil entity using greed to grant you the power of whatever you want, but it locks away your soul. There is good in all of us, but evil will overthrow it if we allow it. Chief Spearhorn once told me holding onto anger is like poison, the longer it sits the stronger it becomes.

This is what happened to Liwanu he wanted power and control so bad, but he allowed the poison inside of him to get worse. Perhaps this has been more than just about Liwanu, this is about all of us freeing them from themselves by expelling the evil. What is in the dark matter? Whatever it is we all were about to find out.

Quickly I asked my uncle Benjamin and Big John to bind me and my brother to pole, and to tie us up fast, Eric thought I was crazy, for this. Benjamin did not want to but Chief Spearhorn nodded to him and said to do it quickly. The look in his eyes were very serious, just like the look he gave my dad that night after the cave incident.

Anai'Lique steadied her arrow in our direction.

"I hope you know what you are doing, I don't want to use these on you,"

I told her just make sure she stays alive, so I don't have to use them on her. She nodded, and kept Aim, I asked her to call out to the others to aim their arrows up toward the sky. With my blood in the bottle, they each dipped their arrowheads in it and took aim. With the release of the arrows the sky lit up like fireworks, the dark matter could no longer be, but it forced out the one we had been waiting for.

Then he appeared to all of us, but why now? Why did it wait to come out in full form? Was it my blood? Or perhaps it was waiting on someone else. Eric said he hoped I knew what I was doing and how could we fight with our hands tied. I told him to trust me and merge our minds together. Then a ghostly white mist snaking along the ground covered out feet then snaked its way up alongside of our bodies.

Whispers of our ancient language spoke as lights circled around us at lightning speed, then. Just as the beast appeared before everyone, my brother and I were merged into one to fight the beast inside the dark matter. The beast known as Liwanu, growled at everyone, scoping out the crowd fixing its eyes on Chief Spearhorn, but Tilileah and Milileah stepped in front of him.

Shifting from beast to man he transformed into Liwanu, looking at both women who were direct descendants of Lei'Liana daughter of Chief Iyotaka. The one Liwanu fell in love with and was angered that she had twin boys that were hidden in fear he would discover them. The women held their ground as he shifted back into beast again and then he went on the attack.

Striking both women, they fell to the ground, others joined in as, they fought the huge beast. Arrows shot into its back, as he grew stronger drinking the blood of those he wounded. They drove him closer to the fire as they attempted to restrain him. Sparks of light flashed as every arrow struck him. Transforming into half human half beast, it was time for my brother and I made our move.

Emerging from the dark matter, we faced him head on, fighting as warriors. We were as a giant tall and strong. Shifting in and out of the darkness with our strengths combined, we did not let him stop us. More and more tribes joined us as we fought to put an end to this generational curse that had plagued us for centuries. This was the end for us if we did not destroy this beast. Chief Spearhorn gathered a chain as we struck the beast to bind him. We fought with all the strength we had, then what felt like an earthquake as a thunderous sound came from the ground.

An army of huge wolves, stood tall as giants formed a circle around us. While others on fours kept watch to make sure the barrier would not be crossed. Anai'Lique and the others stood with arrows ready to fire. They were everywhere. Eric and I stood with our backs to one another ready for the first move. Tilileah and Mileah stood unharmed, as they tossed sage and ash, and spoke a binding spell to keep him from shifting again.

Spotting owl, Benjamin, and Big John held their positions. One of the giant wolves howled at the moon, as to signify their arrival, then more arrived as a thunderous sound shook the ground. We fought this beast with everything we had, I could not let this night end with him being left alive.

With every strike we gave him, he struck us even harder. While getting knocked down, we got back up. Being careful to be bitten, we needed to get the chain around his neck. Eric and I drove the beast back toward the fire, I yelled toward Anai'Lique and told her to get ready. We only had one shot to get the blood in his mouth.

Once in position, she shot her arrow, but our plan failed so the beast charge at her, But Ana'Lique was fearless so she stood her ground. With the first arrow, she struck it in the shoulder, but he kept charging at her. The second arrow, she struck it in the hip. But that did not slow it down either.

The beast kept charging, no one could stop it, Eric and I ran as fast as we could. We watched as the beast leaped into the air right above her, then with the third arrow it struck the beast deep inside its mouth before landing on top her.

The beast gagged, as others removed him from Anai'Lique. We were not sure if she was alive or dead. We needed to remove the beast quickly. Once the beast was removed, Anai'Lique just laid there lifeless, Chief Spearhorn, Dr. Gregory Spears and, Nurse Mei'omi immediately attended to her. Her sign of coughing relieved some of us, others wondered if she too would turn, picking up her bow and arrow I aimed it at her.

"Are you with us?"

As helped her up stand to her feet, Dr. Spears examined her. while catching her breath she gazed at me.

"If I wasn't for you would be dead already."

She walked toward me, as I kept aim.

"You're not holding it right, aim for the chest. Don't worry I am unharmed, I was prepared just in case."

She had taken a potion long before the battle began.

Once Liwanu was subdued I stood before what caused me so much pain, looking into his eyes I saw myself. The anger that I felt of not knowing who or what I was. This man, this beast vowed to kill my people, he killed my birth parents. There had been many stories told that if you catch a Suhnoyee Wah of this kind, keep it bound then bind it for all eternity. But this is not so easily done.

A Navajo Elder stepped forward pointing toward Liwanu and said.

"Yeenaaldlooshi"

Which means skin walker. There are many names for them given from each tribe but since we were all here together, we now can put an end to this nightmare. Some of the wolves moved toward us as Liwanu was once again bound to the pole only this time not as man but as beast. Anai'Lique gave the vial of my blood to Chief Spearhorn, while strong men held the beast with chains. Eric watch the night sky, as others spoke sacred words over the beast. Slowly he began to shift into man, again while still bound.

Chief Spearhorn handed the vial to me and my brother, Eric sliced his palm with a knife to draw blood. He let it drip inside the potion as Chief Spearhorn added the silver powder to it. Once mixed together, a white smoke appeared and together we forced it down the throat of Liwanu. He spit on us and told us we were fools, then as we watch his countenance change, he once again called upon the evil to take him and make him even stronger.

And just as it formed over him. The dark-skinned man emerged from nowhere and held his staff into the dark matter creating an illuminating bright light. That immediately shot through the air lighting up the night sky. The dark entity was swallowed up into his staff, and there it would remain Liwanu let out a cry as a ghostly white mist surrounded him. He stared at me long and hard and said.

"U-la-si-gv-il a-le-ni-do-a na-hna."

Which means Darkness lives on. Then he was gone and so were the wolves. Could this be it? Is it finally over? I looked around to see the sun rising over the mountains. It was over finally, I embraced my brother with a hug and told him he fought well.

Benjamin, Big John also hugged us. Chief Spearhorn said we can all go home in peace now, but he expected me to spend time on the reservation. This night would be recorded in the archives for future generations. Everyone embraced each other singing songs of victory while dancing to the beat of the drums.

It's funny how you spend your life running away from things that seem to end your life. So much was on my mind as we headed back home, Eric decided to stay with me, so we could graduate together. My parents were so grateful to have me back home, Becca was also happy she and Nai'Jae became close as did Ms. Creed and Dr. Morgan. Tony was still Tony and well Elsha and I made it official by dating with permission of her father of course.

Chief Morgan was happy the town had returned peaceful again. I kept in touch with Benjamin and Big John, it felt nice to have my family back.

My mind is still haunted by now faded memories, as time goes by, I find myself staring in the mirror for long periods of time, even the dark. Evil will always be upon this world, but it is what man does with it determines the outcome. I choose to live and not worry about what or who decides to end my life.

Through each generation similar stories are told by each tribe about the night we faced what had stalked us for generations. There are many names for night wolves, but this one will be told forever.

The night the Legend of the Suhnoyee came to an end or did it?

The End.

Printed in the United States
By Bookmasters